Large Print

TAY   Taylor, Jennifer

        Home by Christmas

Maybe the kiss had started out as an accident, but it had gone beyond that stage now.

He kissed her gently and with great tenderness, then drew back and looked at her, knowing that he would remember this moment all his life. Her soft brown hair had started to come free from its elegant chignon and his stomach muscles bunched when he saw how the silky wisps had curled themselves around her small ears.

He lifted a hand, touched one gossamer-fine strand, then breathed in and out just to be certain that he could still do something as mundane as breathe. It felt as though he were having an out-of-body experience, that he was looking down on himself and watching what was happening. Was it real? Had it happened? Had he just kissed Lisa not as a friend but as a lover?

Her eyes suddenly opened and Will felt a wave of panic wash over him when he saw the confusion they held.

What in the name of heaven had he done?

Jennifer Taylor lives in the north-west of England with her husband Bill. She had been writing Mills & Boon® romances for some years, but when she discovered Medical Romances™, she was so captivated by these heart-warming stories that she set out to write them herself! When not writing or doing research for her latest book, Jennifer's hobbies include reading, travel, walking her dog and retail therapy (shopping!). Jennifer claims all the bending and stretching to reach the shelves is the best exercise possible.

Recent titles by the same author:

A FAMILY OF THEIR OWN
HIS BROTHER'S SON
LIFE SUPPORT
MORGAN'S SON
THE BABY ISSUE
ADAM'S DAUGHTER

HOME BY CHRISTMAS

BY
JENNIFER TAYLOR

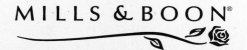

MILLS & BOON®

First published in Great Britain 2002
Large Print edition 2003
Harlequin Mills & Boon Limited,
Eton House, 18-24 Paradise Road,
Richmond, Surrey TW9 1SR

© Jennifer Taylor 2002

ISBN 0 263 17986 9

Set in Times Roman 16¼ on 17½ pt.
17-0603-55613

Printed and bound in Great Britain
by Antony Rowe Ltd, Chippenham, Wiltshire

CHAPTER ONE

'THERE'S something I want to ask you, Lisa. Will you marry me?'

'M-marry you?'

Lisa Bennett's hazel eyes widened as she stared at the man seated across the table from her. They were in the middle of having dinner at Dalverston's newest and most up-market restaurant, The Blossoms, when James had dropped his bombshell. It was two weeks before Christmas and the restaurant was filled to capacity that night. The steady hum of a dozen different conversations filled the elegantly appointed dining room so it was little wonder she was afraid that she might have misheard him.

'Don't look so surprised, darling. Surely you must have realised how I feel about you?' James Cameron reached across the table and took hold of her hand. 'I'm crazy about you, Lisa. Isn't it obvious?'

'I...well...um...' Lisa tried to marshal her thoughts but the announcement had come like a bolt from the blue. *Had* she had an inkling that James felt this way about her?

She searched her heart and sighed as she was forced to admit that there had been a number of signs in recent weeks that his feelings towards her had been deepening. They had met at a mutual friend's birthday party in the summer and had started going out together a short time later. Lisa had deliberately kept their relationship low-key in the beginning, but, if she was honest, she had sensed that James had been starting to want rather more than that. She had simply tried not to think about it because it still made her feel a little guilty to imagine falling in love with another man.

She hurriedly pushed that thought to the back of her mind because there was no point thinking about the past when she had this present situation to deal with. 'I knew that you liked me,' she began hesitantly, then stopped when James laughed.

'It's a bit more than that, my love.' He gave her a rueful smile. 'I like an awful lot of people, but I don't go around asking them to marry me, I assure you!'

'Of course not,' she said hurriedly, wishing that she knew what to say to him.

If only Will was here then she could have asked his advice, she thought wistfully, then sighed again because at some point she would have to stop relying on Will to sort out her problems. She was a grown woman of thirty-three and held down a responsible job as a junior registrar on the children's intensive care unit at Dalverston General Hospital. Surely it shouldn't be beyond her to cope with a proposal of marriage without needing her best friend's advice?

The thought of not being able to turn to Will for help made her feel rather odd for some reason. Fortunately the waiter arrived at that point with the dessert trolley so she took her time choosing what she wanted to give herself a breathing space. By the time a crystal glass filled with white and dark chocolate mousse was placed in front of her, Lisa was feeling a little steadier even though she had no idea what she was going to tell James in answer to his proposal. Did she like him enough to want to spend the rest of her life with him?

'Look, sweetheart, I can tell this has come as a shock to you.' James picked up her hand and kissed her fingertips.

Lisa shivered as a frisson ran through her. She had noticed with increasing frequency how she responded to James's gentle kisses, his tender caresses. It had been reassuring to know that she could still respond to a man because for so long it had felt as though that part of her had died. Maybe her feelings for him were deeper than she had realised?

'It was a surprise,' she admitted, feeling her heart race at the thought. She summoned a smile, deeming it wiser to keep the mood light because she still wasn't sure what her answer was going to be. 'It's not every day that a woman receives a proposal of marriage.'

'I sincerely hope not!' James kissed her fingertips again, grinning when he felt her shiver once more. His expression was far more assured when he continued. 'I would be really worried if you confessed that this was your fourth proposal in as many days.'

'Fat chance of that. I spend my days surrounded by sick children and anxious parents. The only other man I see on a regular basis is Will, and I really and truly can't see Will asking me to marry him!'

James laughed and she followed suit, but there seemed to be a sting in the tail of that statement. Will certainly wouldn't ask her to marry him and she wouldn't expect him to, so what was wrong?

Will was her best friend, the one person in the whole world to whom she could always turn in a crisis. The boundaries of their relationship had been drawn up years ago and romance had never featured in it. Yet for some reason she found herself conjuring up a picture of how Will would look if he'd been sitting across the table from her at that moment.

His dark brown hair would be flopping over his forehead and there would be a smile on his mouth because Will was always smiling. It was one of the reasons why he was the most popular member of Dalverston General's paediatric surgery team. Everyone loved Will—staff, parents and especially the children.

He would be recounting some tale about what one of the children had done and his deep blue eyes would be sparkling with laughter. Naturally, he would have dressed for the occasion because dining out at The Blossoms was an event and ranked high on the 'must go there when I win the lottery' list that was pinned to the staffroom noticeboard. However, Will's ideas on what the well-dressed diner sported wouldn't be *quite* the same as everyone else's.

Lisa swallowed a chuckle as she imagined the mismatched shirt and tie Will would have chosen for the occasion. She'd never been able to decide if he was colour-blind or just plain crazy! She certainly couldn't imagine James wearing the kind of clothes that Will normally wore…

Lisa blinked and once again she was back in the present. She realised immediately that she had missed what James had said while she'd been daydreaming. She struggled to catch up, hoping that he hadn't noticed how abstracted she had been.

'And that's why I don't want you to give me your answer tonight, darling.'

'You don't?' she repeated, mentally filling in what had gone before. He must mean her answer to his proposal, she realised, and breathed a sigh of relief at being let off the hook for the moment.

'No.' He shrugged, his shoulders rising and falling beneath his suit jacket. James was a barrister and favoured the same kind of impeccable clothing out of work as he wore in court.

Lisa found herself thinking that Will didn't even own a suit—he wore sports jackets and trousers to work, and jeans and sweatshirts in his free time—before she forced herself to concentrate on the conversation. However, it was faintly alarming to realise how easily her thoughts kept wandering.

'You need time to think about this, Lisa, and I don't intend to put any pressure on you. I want you to be sure that you feel the same about me as I do about you. That's why I'm hoping that you will agree to spend Christmas with me at the cottage.' He squeezed her hand. 'I think it would help if we spent some time together, don't you?'

Lisa flushed because she understood what he was really saying. James had been very patient and hadn't tried to persuade her to go to bed with him even though she knew that he wanted to sleep with her. However, if she agreed to go to his cottage for Christmas then she would be agreeing to take their relationship a stage further, and maybe it *was* time that she did so, especially now that he had asked her to marry him. Surely, they both needed to be sure that the physical side of their relationship would be as pleasant as the rest?

'I…I think that would be a good idea,' she said huskily, then cleared her throat. It wasn't fair to James to make it appear as though she was agreeing to some sort of dreadful ordeal.

'I'd really love to spend Christmas with you,' she said more firmly, and saw his smile widen with delight.

'I'm so pleased, darling.' He leant across the table to kiss her then suddenly stopped and looked round. 'Hmm, probably not the best place to show you just how thrilled I am!'

Lisa laughed, although she couldn't help feeling a little disappointed by his lack of spontaneity. She dipped her spoon into the delicious chocolate confection in front of her and told herself sternly to stop acting like a child. A lot of James's important clients dined at The Blossoms so who could blame him for not wanting to make a spectacle of himself?

Still, Will wouldn't have done that. He wouldn't have given a damn who had been watching. He would have kissed the woman he loved right there in the middle of the busy restaurant and to hell with what anyone thought.

She frowned. How odd that she kept thinking about Will all the time.

*   *   *

'How's he doing?'

Will Saunders glanced at his colleague, Dave Carson, who was his anaesthetist that night. They were nearing the end of a gruelling five-hour-long operation to remove a metal stake from the abdomen of an eight-year-old boy called Daniel Kennedy.

Daniel had been climbing onto a garage roof to retrieve his football when he had slipped and fallen onto some iron railings. It had taken the emergency services almost two hours to cut him free. Will had gone to the scene of the accident, knowing that it was vital to have some idea what he would be dealing with when he got Daniel back to Theatre.

The metal stake had passed straight through Daniel's abdomen, missing his spinal column by mere fractions of an inch as it had exited through his back. It had caused extensive tissue and nerve damage, and severely damaged his large intestine, too. Just dealing with the massive amount of blood which the child had lost had been a major headache, and then there had been all the problems of realigning the torn muscles and blood vessels to stitch them back into place.

Infection would be their next, biggest obstacle to overcome, but Will knew that he mustn't look too far ahead. He had to focus on doing his job to the very best of his ability and leave the rest to his colleagues. It would take a team effort to pull the child through this ordeal.

'He's holding his own, but I'd be happier if you speeded things up,' Dave replied laconically from the head of the operating table. 'You'd think you would be a lot quicker at sewing up after all the practice you've had, Will.'

'Oh, he's not as slow as some I could mention.' Madge Riley, the Theatre sister, cut into the conversation. 'You should try working with Dr Maxwell and then you'd know what slow really means. It took him almost an hour to sew up after that emergency appendicectomy this morning. His hands were shaking so hard that he dropped the needle twice!'

'Give the poor guy a break, Madge,' Will exhorted. He waggled his eyebrows at her over the top of his mask. 'You know he's all fingers and thumbs because he's got a bit of a *thing* about you.'

'Can I help it if I have this effect on the younger men in the department?' Madge retorted, batting her eyelashes at him. Plump, grey-haired and on the wrong side of fifty, she kept threatening to retire, only she never quite got round to writing her letter of resignation. She was a superb nurse, though, and Will knew they were fortunate to have her working with them.

'Who said it was only the younger men who appreciated your charms?' he replied, his blue eyes glinting with laughter when she pulled a face at him.

He put a final stitch into the section of tissue he had been working on and nodded. 'Right, that should do it. We'll leave the wound open and pack it with gauze until we're sure there's no sign of infection setting in, although I doubt we'll be that lucky. Lord only knows what might have been on that lump of metalwork.'

He glanced at the chunk of iron railing which he had extracted from Daniel's body, thinking how amazing it was that the boy had survived this far. Now they would have to wait and see if he would pull through but, what with the blood loss and shock, the tissue damage and high risk of infection, the odds certainly seemed to be stacked against him.

Will tried to shrug off a momentary feeling of inadequacy as he left Theatre. It stemmed mainly from tiredness because an operation as complex as this one, coming on top of a full day's work, was bound to have been draining. However, he knew that it wasn't the only reason why he felt so flat. Lisa had been going out with James Cameron tonight and, try as he may, he couldn't shake off the feeling that there had been a reason why Cameron had taken her to The Blossoms for dinner. Was Cameron hoping that an expensive meal might persuade her into his bed, perhaps?

Will swore softly as he kicked open the door to the changing room. What business was it of his, anyway? Lisa was free to do whatever she chose, and if he was a true friend then he should be pleased that she had reached a point whereby she would consider having a relationship with another man.

She had been devastated when Gareth had been killed in that tragic skiing accident during their last year at med school together. Gareth had been an accomplished skiier but even he had been unable to do anything when a novice—who shouldn't have been on the advanced piste—had careered into him and knocked him off course. The Swiss police had explained that

Gareth would have died instantly when he had hit the tree.

It had been Will who had flown out to Switzerland to identify his friend and bring him home, and Will who had made all the arrangements for Gareth's funeral. Gareth's elderly parents lived in Australia and had been too frail to make the journey to England, and Lisa had been far too upset to deal with it.

Her grief had known no bounds and Will had felt completely helpless as he had tried to comfort her. At one point he had feared that she would never get over Gareth's death, in fact. She had dropped out of college without sitting her final exams and he had honestly believed that she would give up medicine altogether. It had been almost two years before she had gone back to complete her studies, and in all that time Will had done his best to help and support her, spending long hours listening as she had talked about the plans she and Gareth had made for the future.

Gareth had been his best friend as well as Lisa's fiancé and Will had wanted to help in any way that he could. He had promised himself after the funeral that he would do everything in his power to make sure Lisa was happy for Gareth's sake. That was why he had invited her to share his flat when she had taken the job at Dalverston General, because it had meant that he would be around if she needed help.

Now it looked as though she was finally getting her life together and he should be glad about it, not feeling as though he were about to lose something more precious than life itself. Lisa had never been his in the first place so he couldn't lose her.

That thought just depressed him all the more so Will decided not to think about it as he shed his scrub suit and headed for the showers. The water was hot and he turned on the jets to full power, groaning half in pleasure but mostly in pain as the water pounded the aching muscles in his neck and shoulders. He'd spent most of the day in Theatre, plus a large chunk of the night, and his body was paying for the long hours spent bending over the operating table.

He turned off the water at last and briskly towelled himself dry then went back to the changing room to get dressed. He was just taking his shirt off a hanger when there was a tap on the door and he looked round to find Lisa peering in at him.

'Can I come in?' she asked, hovering uncertainly in the doorway.

'Of course. I'm more or less decent.' He grabbed the shirt, feeling oddly uncomfortable about her seeing him half-dressed. Bearing in mind that they often bumped into one another coming out of the bathroom in the flat it seemed very strange, but he couldn't help it.

He quickly buttoned the shirt then pulled a tie from the rail. He glanced round when Lisa gave a choked little laugh. 'What?'

'Do you really think that tie goes with the shirt, Will?' she asked, a smile curving her mouth. She lifted warm hazel eyes to his and Will felt something inside him clench like a tightly bunched fist so that he had to force himself to breathe in then out before he could speak.

'I don't know,' he said, staring helplessly at the tie while he tried to work out what was wrong with him. Was he having some sort of asthma attack, perhaps? Or had he developed a touch of angina? There was a definite pain in his chest and there was no doubt that breathing seemed to be a lot more difficult than it normally was. It was an effort to focus on the question Lisa had asked him when he felt so confused.

'What's wrong with it exactly?'

'It's green—*bright* green—and your shirt is blue.' She shrugged and once again he felt that iron fist grip his vital organs as he saw her small breasts rise and fall beneath her blue silk blouse. 'They…well…sort of clash.'

'Do they?' he muttered, dragging his eyes away and sucking in another desperate lungful of air which felt as turgid as steam. What on earth was going on? Why was he suddenly noticing things like *that*? He was Lisa's friend and a friend certainly shouldn't be having lustful thoughts about her body!

He cleared his throat, overwhelmed by a feeling of self-loathing. 'I hadn't realised they didn't go together. They look OK to me.'

'Obviously.' She gave him a quick grin them reached into the locker and took out a dark blue tie with a discreet cream leaf pattern sprinkled all over it. 'Try this and see what you think.'

Will took it simply because he didn't care one way or the other. What difference did it make what colour tie he wore when his whole world seemed to be hurtling out of control? He knotted the tie and turned down the shirt-collar but his hands were trembling and the tiny buttons that held it in place defeated his attempts to fasten them.

Lisa is my friend, he repeated desperately, but for some reason the words didn't sound the same as they had done in the past.

'Here, let me do that, butterfingers.'

Before he could summon up an aye, a yes or a no, she had stepped in front of him and briskly begun to fasten the buttons for him. Will held himself rigid, terrified that he would do something crazy like put his arms around her.

That was what he wanted to do—put his arms around her and hold her close—and although he'd done it a thousand times in the past when he had been trying to comfort her, he knew it wouldn't be the same if he did it now. He wanted to hold her now because all of a sudden his arms felt empty without her in them. He wanted to fill them with her and know that she needed him as much as he needed her...

'There! What do you think? Isn't that better?'

Will blinked and the delightful little scenario that had been unwinding inside his head switched itself off. All of a sudden he was back to reality and the reality was that he was Lisa's friend and if he hoped to remain so he could never, *ever* take her in his arms the way he had been longing to do.

'Um, yep, that's much better, isn't it?' He summoned a smile as he turned to peer into the tiny mirror set into the door of the locker, but he couldn't deny how shaken he felt by what had happened.

'Liar! Admit it, Will, you can't see any difference whatsoever, can you?' she demanded, glaring at him in a way that made him wonder what was wrong with her. Why on earth should it matter so much if he preferred her choice of necktie to his?

'Not really,' he confessed, his deep blue eyes searching her face for a clue to what was really going on. Something had obviously upset her and he had no idea what it could be until a thought suddenly occurred to him. A rush of anger hit him and he straightened abruptly, so abruptly, in fact, that he saw her take a step back.

'I was only joking, Will…' she began, but he shook his head.

'Forget the tie. It doesn't matter. What's happened, Lisa? I can tell something is wrong.'

He reached for her hands, although he had to make a conscious effort not to grip them too hard as the anger inside him grew to gigantic proportions. If Cameron had tried to *force* her to go to bed with him…!

'Not wrong exactly.' She gave a wistful sigh and his heart spasmed with pain because he couldn't bear to hear her sounding so troubled.

'Why don't you tell me what's wrong and then we can see if we can sort it all out,' he said more gently this time.

He let his hands slide to her wrists, feeling the steady beat of her pulse beneath his fingers. Its rhythm was a little faster than normal but not so fast that it alarmed him unduly, and he realised that he might have jumped to conclusions. Maybe Cameron had been the perfect gentleman and there was something else worrying her? He was just about to urge her to tell him when she spoke.

'James asked me to marry him tonight and I'm not sure what to do.'

She looked up and Will felt something inside him shrivel up in terror when he saw the plea in her eyes. 'I need you to help me make up my mind, Will. Do you think I should marry him?'

*   *   *

Lisa held her breath. Deep down she knew it was wrong to ask Will to help her make a decision like this, but she needed his advice more than ever. Will was always so clear in his views and she knew she could trust him to tell her the truth. If he didn't believe that James was the right man for her, he would say so.

A frown pleated her brow. Surely she shouldn't need anyone to tell her that? She should know in her heart whether or not James was the man she wanted to marry. But she had fallen into the habit of relying on Will to help her make any important decisions about her personal life. When it came to work then she had no such problems; she was always decisive in that area of her life. It bothered her to realise how dependent she was on him outside work, but it was too late to have second thoughts.

'I really don't think that's a question I can answer, Lisa.'

She jumped when he spoke, wondering why his voice sounded so harsh all of a sudden. There was none of the usual warmth and friendly concern in it that she had come to expect.

She shot him an uncertain look but Will was taking his jacket out of his locker and she couldn't see his expression. It left her feeling rather as though she were floundering in the middle of the ocean without a lifeline to cling to, and it was a feeling she hated. Ever since Gareth had died Will had been there for her, her rock, her lifeline.

'I just wanted your advice, that's all,' she said quickly. 'I know you can't make up my mind for me.'

She gave a tinkly little laugh then grimaced when she realised how false it had sounded. 'Sorry. It came as a bolt from the blue, to be honest. I never expected James to ask me to marry him so I'm not sure whether I'm coming or going at the moment.'

'Which is why you decided I might be able to help?'

His tone was so flat that Lisa knew at once that he had deliberately removed any trace of emotion from it. The idea shocked her so much that she stared at him in amazement.

Will *never* tried to hide his feelings, mainly because he was so good-tempered there was no need for him to do so. His calm and equanimity were legendary amongst the staff at Dalverston General. He was always helpful, always caring, always...always just Will! The nicest, kindest, most compassionate man she had ever met. So what was wrong with him now? Was he upset at the thought of her marrying James?

The thought made her pulse race so that it was an effort to act as though everything was fine. 'Yes. Who better to turn to for advice than my dearest friend?'

'Thank you. At least you didn't say your *oldest* friend.'

He treated her to one of his wonderfully warm smiles and Lisa gave herself a brisk mental shake. Of course Will wasn't upset by the idea of her getting married! She was letting her imagination run away with her because it had been a stressful evening. And yet the nagging feeling that something had changed in their relationship wouldn't be dismissed. It was a relief when he looped a friendly arm around her shoulders and steered her towards the door.

'How about we go to the café while we talk this through? I'm suffering from a serious drop in my blood-sugar levels and need a booster before I can think clearly.'

'Sounds good to me,' she said, eagerly grasping at the return to normality.

She smiled up at him and suddenly realised how tired he looked, although it was hardly sur-

prising after the day he'd had. She had bumped
into Madge in the corridor and heard all about
the operation Will had carried out on the boy.
That kind of complex surgery was both physically and mentally draining and it made Lisa
feel guilty all of a sudden about having dumped
her problems on him.

She turned to him and her hazel eyes were
full of concern. 'I really appreciate the offer,
Will, but if you're too tired to deal with this
tonight, then say so. It will keep until another
time.'

'I'm sure it will, but we may as well try to
sort things out while we have the chance.' He
shrugged, although she couldn't help noticing
how he avoided looking at her as he opened the
door. 'I doubt if you'll get much sleep if you're
churning everything round in your head all
night, will you, Lisa?'

'No-o...'

'That's what I thought.' He stepped aside and
bowed and once again the old Will was back,
ready and willing to take charge. 'After you,
madame. Bacon and eggs coming right up, with
a side order of good advice to go with them!'

Lisa chuckled as she led the way from the
room. It was good to know that Will was there

when she needed him. She made her way to the lift and pressed the button then felt her heart lurch as a thought suddenly occurred to her.

If she married James then she couldn't keep turning to Will for advice. It wouldn't be right. And yet the thought of him no longer playing a major role in her life felt wrong somehow, strange.

She summoned a smile as Will came to join her because she didn't want him to guess there was anything wrong. But the nagging little thought wouldn't go away.

She simply couldn't imagine not having Will around.

CHAPTER TWO

THEY went to their usual haunt, a transport café on the bypass. A lot of the staff from the hospital went there after they finished work at night and didn't have the energy to make themselves a meal. Will parked his car in a gap between a couple of lorries and switched off the engine.

'Bacon and eggs for two, is it? Or are you still full from your expensive dinner?'

'The food was delicious, but the portions they serve there are *tiny*.' Lisa grimaced. 'I didn't like to ask the waiter if I could have a bread roll in case James thought I was being greedy!'

'Still at the stage of wanting to make a good impression, are you?' Will said lightly, getting out of the car. He made his way round to join her, praying that he wouldn't make a complete hash of things. Lisa was depending on him to give her some calm and rational advice yet he had never felt less calm or less rational in his entire life.

What the hell was he going to do if she married Cameron? How was he going to fill the void in his life? All of a sudden the future spread out before him and all he could see in it was loneliness. Without Lisa to think about, to worry about and care for, then he had no reason to get up of a morning.

He sighed when it struck him how melodramatic that was. Didn't he have a job he loved, dozens of friends *and* his family? He had everything a man could wish for with one notable exception, i.e. a wife, but now that it looked as though his obligation to Gareth was coming to an end then he could focus on his future. He'd always planned to have children at some point and once Lisa was settled then he could set about finding the right woman to have them with.

The thought should have cheered him up but it didn't. He couldn't seem to see past the bad bits—the fact that Lisa might soon be leaving him—let alone focus on the good. It worried him that he seemed so ambivalent about the idea of her finding happiness when his main aim and objective for the past five years had been to bring that about.

A muggy wall of heat hit them as they en-
tered the café. Will waved as Al, the owner,
shouted a greeting. The place was packed but
they managed to find a table in the corner and
sat down. Al came over to take their order,
bringing with him two huge mugs of wickedly
strong tea.

Will grinned as he picked up the glass can-
ister of sugar and poured a small mountain of
grains into his mug. 'I wonder how long this
has been stewing for?'

Lisa took a sip and shuddered. 'At least a
week from the taste of it. It's pure tannin.'

'Just what I need to give me a lift.' He took
a long swallow of the tea then put his mug
down on the Formica-topped table. 'So, tell me
all about your evening. What was the restaurant
like?'

'Classy. All crisp white tablecloths and
starched napkins, discreetly attentive waiters—
you know the sort of thing.'

She gave a small shrug as she slipped off her
jacket and draped it over the back of her chair.
Once again Will felt that funny sensation grip
his vitals as he watched her smoothing the la-
pels of her blouse and unwittingly drawing his
gaze to the shadowy V of her cleavage.

He dropped his eyes to the table, praying that she hadn't noticed him staring. He had no idea why he was acting like this, but it couldn't have happened at a worse time. Lisa wanted to tell him about Cameron's proposal. She needed his advice about whether or not she should accept it and he couldn't afford to have his mind cluttered up by extraneous thoughts. And yet it was proving incredibly difficult to rid himself of them when he seemed to be aware of her in a way he had never been before.

'Will? Are you all right?'

He jumped when she leant across the table and tapped him on the arm. It was an effort to fix a carefree smile to his face when it felt as though all the worries of the world had suddenly descended on him.

'Fine. I'm probably a bit spaced out after the operation tonight. It was a bit of a stinker, to be honest.'

'I ran into Madge and she told me about it.' She grimaced as she stirred her tea. 'It sounded horrendous. Madge said that the boy was lucky to have survived long enough for you to get him back to hospital.'

'It was pretty nasty,' he agreed. 'I've rarely seen so much soft-tissue damage. Our biggest headache now is going to be dealing with any infection.'

'That's where we come in.' She smiled at him and her hazel eyes were warm with understanding. 'You can't do everything, Will. You've done the really difficult bit and now you have to leave it up to us to sort out the rest. We'll take good care of him, I promise you.'

'I know you will. Daniel couldn't be in better hands,' he replied sincerely.

Lisa's job in the paediatric intensive care unit meant that a lot of the children he dealt with came under her care. He knew how dedicated she was to her work, and that it wasn't just a job to her. She lavished an awful lot of love on the children she treated, gave each and every one that extra bit of support.

She would make the most wonderful mother, he found himself thinking, then quickly clamped down on that thought because it was of very little relevance. If and when Lisa ever had a family then he would be well off the scene.

The thought was so mind-numbingly painful that he found he could no longer speak and a small silence developed. Fortunately, Al arrived with their order and Will was grateful for the interruption. He had never felt in the least ill at ease around Lisa before but he felt so that night and it worried him. What on earth was going on? Surely he should be pleased for her, instead of feeling as though the bottom had dropped out of his world?

It was too unsettling to try and work out any answers so he applied himself to his meal, hoping it would help if he got some food inside him. It had been hours since he'd last eaten so maybe he hadn't been so far off track when he'd claimed to be suffering from low blood sugar.

They ate in silence until every last scrap had gone. Will heaved a sigh of contentment as he plucked a paper napkin from the dispenser and wiped his mouth. 'I might just live, although it was touch and go at one point, I can tell you.'

'I know what you mean,' she assured him, then grinned when he raised his eyes. 'OK, I know I've just dined at Dalverston's finest restaurant, but it always makes me feel hungry whenever I'm stressed.'

'And you're feeling stressed tonight because Cameron asked you to marry him?' he said quietly, knowing that he couldn't put off the moment any longer.

He settled back in his chair, praying that she couldn't tell how mixed up he was feeling. Of course he wanted to help her reach the right decision, but he wasn't convinced that any advice he offered would be totally unbiased. And yet what did he have against Cameron?

The man was an upstanding pillar of the community. He was rich, successful and unmarried—a real catch, as Will's own mother would have put it. If he'd been asked to compile a list of eligible suitors for Lisa then Cameron would have featured on it, and yet— and *yet*—the thought of her marrying the man stuck in his throat like a nasty dose of indigestion.

'Yes. It was such a surprise. I had no idea...' She broke off and sighed. 'That's not quite true, actually. I did realise that James was...well, attracted to me, but I tried not to think about it. It made me feel a bit guilty, you see.'

A wash of soft colour ran up her face and under cover of the table Will's hands clenched. It was an effort to force out a single word let alone a whole sentence as his mind played tag with the way in which Cameron was *attracted* to her.

'You mean it made you feel guilty because of Gareth?' His voice sounded somewhat strangled when it emerged, and he saw Lisa shoot him an unhappy look.

'You think it's wrong to encourage him, don't you? I can tell. You think I should remain faithful to Gareth's memory?'

'No, I don't think any such thing!' he exploded, realising that he was in danger of undoing years of hard work by acting like an idiot.

Making Lisa understand that she couldn't live solely on her memories had been his main objective since Gareth had died. He knew it was what Gareth would have wanted so week after week, month after month, he'd tried to convince her that she had to think about the future instead of the past. Lisa deserved to find love and happiness again with a man, even if that man wasn't him.

The thought almost blew him away because he had never for a second entertained the idea before. His feelings for Lisa were based on friendship, not...not *sexual* attraction! And yet when he looked at her sitting there across the table from him it wasn't only friendship he felt but a whole lot of other things as well.

It was as though the blinkers had been removed from his eyes and all of a sudden he was seeing her not as Gareth's fiancée but the most beautiful and desirable woman he had ever known.

Hell and damnation! What a time for something like *this* to happen.

'So you don't think it's wrong?' Lisa said uncertainly when she saw the grim expression on Will's face. She wasn't sure what the matter was with him that night but he seemed to be acting very strangely, snapping at her that way. She couldn't recall Will ever speaking to her so sharply before.

Just for a second she found herself wishing that she hadn't gone to find him after James had dropped her off at home. She'd felt so keyed-up by what had happened that she'd needed to talk everything through with him, but maybe it had been a mistake, after all. Maybe Will was growing tired of sorting out her problems, becoming resentful of her constant demands on his time?

A feeling of dread knotted her throat and she swallowed. She couldn't bear to think that she had become a nuisance to him but the facts had to be faced. Will had his own life to lead so why should he want to devote so much time to her all the time? It was hard to hide how upsetting she found that idea when he suddenly spoke.

'I don't think you should feel guilty about what's happened, Lisa. That's just plain silly and you know it is.'

The gentle understanding in his voice made her eyes prickle with tears and she stared at her cup. 'Do I?' she murmured, then looked up when he laughed, that wonderful, warm, *Will* laugh.

'Uh-huh! You're being a complete and utter idiot,' he assured her, tilting back his chair and grinning at her.

Lisa summoned a smile. 'Not that you are trying to insult me, of course.'

'Would I ever?'

His tone was teasing but beneath the laughter she could hear the concern. Will had sensed she was upset and he was trying to make her feel better. It made her see just how very special their friendship was.

'Look, Lisa, you have to take this a step at a time and think it all through.' He let his chair snap back onto all four legs and leant across the table towards her.

Lisa felt the strangest sensation flow through her as she caught the full force of his brilliant blue stare. She could feel heat flowing through her veins, making her heart race and her breathing quicken. Will must have looked at her a million times before but she couldn't remember it having this kind of an effect on her...

'Lisa? Are you listening to me?'

She jumped when he touched her hand and the warm feeling promptly evaporated, much to her relief. Her feelings for Will had always been clearly defined and she didn't want anything to change. Will was her best friend, the person she trusted most in the whole world. She needed that one constant to cling to when everything else was altering with such speed.

'Sorry. As I said, this came as rather a shock even though I knew that James was rather keen on me.'

'And how do you feel, Lisa? Are you *keen* on him, too?'

She pulled a face when she heard the teasing note in his voice. 'All right, I know that sounded a bit wet and like something out of a nineteen-twenties film, but you know what I mean.'

'Oh, I do, old girl!' This time he was openly laughing at her and Lisa sighed.

'You are an absolute pain, Will Saunders! Here am I trying to discuss the most important decision of my entire life and you're making fun of me.'

'Sorry, old bean,' he retorted, before he suddenly sobered. 'But you're right, of course. This really isn't a joking matter. So, seriously, how do you feel about Cameron? Do you think you're in love with him or what?'

'I don't know. That's the honest answer.'

She picked up a spoon and stirred her tea again, wondering why she felt so uncomfortable all of a sudden. She'd never had any difficulty discussing her feelings with Will in the past but she felt awkward about doing so now. 'I like James a lot. He's charming, attentive, kind and good-looking. He's also been very patient about…'

She broke off, wishing with all her heart that she hadn't said that last little bit. Did she really want to discuss the fact that James hadn't tried to persuade her to go to bed with him?

'About you not sleeping with him?' Will touched her hand, just lightly with the tip of his index finger, and smiled at her. 'Hey, this is me you're talking to, Lisa. You don't need to be embarrassed.'

'I'm not,' she said quickly, although it wasn't true. She *was* embarrassed about it, as much embarrassed by the idea of Will knowing that she hadn't slept with James as she would have been if she had done so, and she couldn't understand why she should feel that way. Why should it matter if Will knew about her sex life or, rather, the lack of one?

She hurried on, not wanting to delve too deeply into that question for some reason. 'James has been wonderful about it. Not many men would have been so considerate, in fact,' she said, wanting Will to know how much she appreciated James's forbearance.

'That's good to hear,' he said evenly. He picked up his mug and drank some of his tea then put the cup back on the table. And there was something almost too studied about the way he set it down exactly in the middle of the damp ring it had left on the Formica surface.

Lisa frowned as she saw what he had done. She had the funniest feeling that Will was deliberately keeping a check on himself, watching everything he said and did. It was so out of character for him to behave that way that she couldn't work out what was the matter with him. Unless Will had serious misgivings about her marrying James and was afraid to say so?

'Yes, it is,' she replied, trying not to let him see how unsettled she felt by the idea. Maybe it was silly to set too much store by Will's opinion but she couldn't help it. 'However, I can't expect James to wait for ever. Especially not after he has asked me to marry him.'

'So what's the plan, then?' Will said a shade gruffly.

Lisa shot him an uncertain look but he was stirring his tea. It should have made it easier to tell him what she was planning on doing, but all of a sudden she discovered that her heart was racing. How would Will feel about James's invitation?

'James has asked me to spend Christmas with him at his cottage. I…I think it would be a good idea, don't you?'

Will could hear a buzzing in his ears. It seemed to be getting louder so that he couldn't hear what else Lisa said, although it wouldn't have mattered if he had. His mind seemed to have stalled on that last question and he had to fight back a slightly hysterical laugh.

Lisa wanted him to give her a nice, tidy, *logical* answer when logic didn't enter into this. What this all boiled down to was feelings— how *he* felt about the idea of her spending Christmas with Cameron at his cottage and sleeping with him in his bed. Words couldn't begin to describe how gut-wrenchingly painful he found the idea!

'Will, your beeper!'

He nearly shot out of his chair when she shook his arm. He'd been so immersed in his own agony that he hadn't had a clue that the buzzing sound had been coming from his pocket. He dug out his beeper and checked the display, grimacing when he saw from the code that it was Theatre trying to get in contact with him.

'Looks like I'm needed,' he explained, hunting in the other pocket for his cellphone.

He quickly put through a call, feeling like the lowest form of pond-life as he eagerly agreed when a junior registrar from the general surgical team asked if he would mind returning to the hospital to deal with an emergency admis-

sion. The fact that he could feel relieved because there was a child in urgent need of his
help filled him with disgust, but he couldn't
help it. He desperately didn't want to have to
discuss Lisa's dilemma any more that night, let
alone come up with an answer for her.

'I'll have to go,' he explained, briskly standing and taking his coat off the back of the chair.

'Emergency?' she asked, quickly following
suit. She slid her arms into her jacket, mur-
muring her thanks when Will picked up her bag
and handed it to her.

'A four-year-old girl who's fallen out of an
upstairs window. Multiple fractures,' he told
her, swiftly heading for the door. They had almost reached it when he realised that he hadn't
paid their bill.

He stopped and hunted through his pockets
again, groaning when all he came up with was
a handful of loose change and a button that had
come off his jacket weeks ago. He'd intended
to go to the cash machine on his way home,
but he'd not had a chance once he'd received
the call about Daniel Kennedy.

'I've no cash on me,' he explained. 'I meant
to get some on the way home. Maybe Al will

put it on the slate and I can pay him the next time I'm in?'

'Don't worry. I'll get it,' Lisa said, quickly taking her wallet from her bag. She went to the counter and Will heard her laugh at some comment Al passed.

He waited by the door while she made her way back across the room. It was warm in the café that night and the heat had added a touch of colour to her face and there seemed to be a definite sparkle in her eyes as well. It was a long time since he had seen her looking so animated, in fact, although her vivacity had been one of the first things he had noticed when Gareth had introduced them.

Lisa had been full of fun back then. It had only been after Gareth's death that she had grown sombre and quiet, sad. Now it was both a pleasure and a pain to see her looking more like she used to do because he understood the reason for it.

She looked different tonight because she was looking towards the future at last. It was painful to know that he hadn't been able to give her back her sparkle and that another man had.

'Al said to tell you that he likes your style. He's all in favour of women footing the bill in these days of equality.'

Will managed a sickly smile but the thought that he could be guilty of such a dog-in-the-manger attitude didn't sit easily with him. 'I hope you told him that I'm noted for my views on the equality of the sexes?'

'Oh, sure! So that's why you wouldn't let me paint the living-room ceiling the other week and insisted that you should do it instead? Come on, Will, you know very well that you could no more treat a woman as your equal when it comes to doing something dangerous than you could fly to the moon!'

'If you'd really wanted to paint the ceiling yourself then you should have said so,' he said stiffly. He opened the door and pulled up the collar of his jacket as a blast of icy December air hit them.

Lisa grinned as she huddled into her jacket. 'I didn't—not really. And don't go all prickly on me, because I wasn't getting at you. You have this overwhelming need to protect everyone, Will, and I for one wouldn't want you to change.'

'Sure?' he asked, wondering why it seemed so important to know that she was telling him the truth.

'One hundred per cent certain. I like you just the way you are, Will Saunders. Warts and all!'

She slid her hand through his arm and reached up on tiptoe to kiss his cheek. It was the sort of kiss they had exchanged countless times in the past and yet it had the most gal-vanising effect on him that night.

Will didn't have a clue that he was going to turn until he suddenly found they were facing each other. Lisa was still standing on tiptoe, her hand still resting on his arm, but her lips had skidded from his cheek when he'd turned and somehow ended up at the corner of his mouth. It was the easiest thing in the world to turn his head another fraction of an inch...

Will stifled a groan when he felt the softness of her lips make contact with his. His head spun as he became aware of a dozen different things all at once, like how sweet her hair smelled, how quickly she was breathing, how huge and bright her eyes looked as she stared up at him.

Her lids suddenly lowered and he felt a surge of something hot and wild race through him when she moved just a little so that their mouths settled more firmly together. Maybe the kiss had started out as an accident but it had gone beyond that stage now.

He kissed her gently and with great tenderness then drew back and looked at her, knowing that he would remember this moment all his life. She looked so beautiful as she stood there with her eyes closed and her lips parted, her delicate oval face upturned to his. Her soft brown hair had started to come free from its elegant chignon and his stomach muscles bunched when he saw how the silky wisps had curled themselves around her small ears.

He lifted a hand, touched one gossamer-fine strand then breathed in and out just to be certain that he could still do something as mundane as breathe. It felt as though he were having an out-of-body experience, that he was looking down on himself and watching what was happening.

Was it real? Had it happened? Had he just kissed Lisa not as a friend but as a lover?

Her eyes suddenly opened and Will felt a wave of panic wash over him when he saw the confusion they held.

What in the name of heaven had he done?

CHAPTER THREE

'WILL, I...'

'Sorry! I didn't realise the ground was so slippery. Mind you, it's cold enough tonight to freeze, isn't it?'

Lisa blinked then looked uncertainly at the ground. There was indeed a shimmer of frost on the tarmac so was Will saying that he had *slipped* and that was how they had ended up kissing one another?

She tested out the theory, trying to spot the flaws in it, but deep down she wanted to believe him. She wanted to believe that the kiss had been pure accident and not design because it was less scary to do so. If it *had* been an accident then they could carry on as normal. But if it hadn't then she would have to decide what to do about it. How did she really feel about the idea of Will kissing her as a lover rather than as a friend?

The question brought a rush of heat to her face and she turned away before he could notice. 'Apology accepted,' she said huskily, starting off across the car park as though she were being hotly pursued by demons.

Will kept pace with her, whistling under his breath in a way that should have been soothing yet which made her nerves jangle all the more. Was he behaving just a bit *too* casually perhaps, trying too hard to act as though nothing had happened?

Lisa shot him a wary look as he unlocked the car but he didn't look as though he was trying to hide anything. She slid into the passenger seat, feeling almost weak with relief. The kiss had been an accident. Will must have slipped and somehow their mouths had met and...

And did that also explain why it had been so wonderful that her knees had started knocking again just because she'd been thinking about it?

Lisa bit her lip, terrified that she might blurt out something unforgivable. Maybe the kiss had been wonderful but there was no way that she wanted her relationship with Will to change. She had enough to contend with at the moment, what with James's proposal and his suggestion that she should spend Christmas with him. Will was Will and her feelings for him were ones of friendship. End of story. He felt exactly the same about her.

Didn't he?

'I'll drop you off at the flat then go straight back to work. Heaven knows what time I'll get in so don't bolt the door on me.'

'What? Oh, no, of course not.' She hurriedly summoned a smile when he glanced at her, but that last question was giving her hot and cold chills. Will felt nothing but friendship for her. He certainly didn't fancy her. And yet the thought stubbornly refused to die.

'Typical that this should happen tonight,' she said quickly, in the hope that it might help to think about something else. 'You've had one difficult case and now it looks as though you've got another right on top of it.'

'A bit like buses—they tend to come in twos,' he replied, turning into the forecourt of the block of flats where they lived. He drew up outside the front door while she hunted for her keys. 'What time are you on duty tomorrow?'

'Six.' She grimaced as she jangled the key fob in her palm. 'I hate earlies, especially when I've been out the night before.'

'Well, I'll try not to disturb you when I come in.' He checked his watch and groaned. 'Is that the time already? I had no idea it had gone midnight. You'd better get to bed.'

'Shame you can't come, too,' she said without thinking, then felt herself cringe when she realised how suggestive that must have sounded.

She hastily got out of the car and waved as Will drove away, but the fact that she had even paused to consider what she'd said to him made her feel even more mixed up. Since when had she needed to be aware of any sexual innuendo creeping into their conversation? But that had been before Will had kissed her. Had it really been an accident, as he had claimed?

Lisa sighed as she let herself into the building. She was in serious danger of building a mountain out of the proverbial molehill if she didn't stop this right away. Will had explained what had happened and when had he ever lied to her?

Of all the half-baked excuses to come up with, that one should win an award!

Will scooped a handful of Hibiscrub from the dispenser and lathered his forearms. He was in the process of scrubbing up before the operation, a task that left his mind free to wander where it chose. The fact that it kept coming back to that moment in the car park when he had claimed it had been the icy conditions underfoot that had caused him to kiss Lisa made him grind his teeth with shame.

What sane person came up with a story like that? She was bound to see through it, guaranteed to spot it as the snivelling lie it was, and then what would he do? How could he hope to explain why he had kissed her like that when he had no idea himself?

'There is being thorough and being masochistic. Give yourself a break, Will. Whatever sin you've committed, it can't be that bad.'

Will looked round when Dave nudged him sharply in the ribs. He grimaced when he saw the anaesthetist shoot a meaningful look at his reddened forearms. 'Oh, I've got a lot on my mind at the moment. Take no notice.'

'Really? Well, there's only one reason I know of that reduces a healthy male mind to pure mush: a woman. Am I right or am I right?'

Dave turned to Madge before Will could say anything. 'Did you know that our Will has some woman on the go? It looks as though she's leading him a bit of a dance, too, from the pitiful state he's in.'

'And here was I thinking that you were faithful only to me,' Madge declared sadly, shaking out a sterile towel and handing it to Will. 'So who is she, then? She must be a looker if she's replaced me in your affections.'

'She's no one,' he said quickly, then realised his mistake when Dave smirked. 'What I meant is that there is no woman,' he said curtly. 'It's all down to Dave's overly fertile imagination.'

'If you say so,' Madge replied, winking at Dave as she handed him a towel as well. 'We'll believe you, won't we, Dr Carson?'

'Of course we will,' Dave agreed, completely deadpan. 'Did you happen to see those fairies in the corridor on your way in, Madge? There were at least a dozen of them from what I could count.'

'And there were half a dozen elves as well…'

'Oh, ha-ha, very funny!' Will glowered as the pair dissolved into fits of laughter. 'You two have missed your vocation. You would have made a superb music-hall act. Now, if we have finished with the jokes, boys and girls, maybe we can get started?'

'Aye, aye, sir.' Dave snapped to attention and saluted. He headed towards the anteroom where their patient was waiting, whispering to Madge in a loud aside that was meant to be heard, 'I'll find out who she is, Madge. Trust me.'

Will chose to ignore them as he went into Theatre to get ready, but he couldn't deny that Dave's parting comment had worried him. The thought that people might make the connection and realise that it was Lisa who was causing him so much soul-searching gave him hot and cold chills. It made him see that he had to nip this in the bud. Lisa was his friend and once he got that fact firmly re-established in his mind, there wouldn't be a problem.

It all sounded so easy in theory, but as Dave wheeled in their patient Will knew in his heart it could never be that simple. How could he go back to thinking of Lisa purely as a friend after what had happened that night?

The little girl's injuries were so severe that Will knew from the outset there was little chance of saving her. She had fallen thirty feet onto concrete flags and there wasn't a bone in her small body that hadn't been smashed. He did everything he could, working on long after he knew it was hopeless, but she was just too badly injured to be saved.

The silence in the operating theatre was tes-
timony to the toll it took on the staff when they
lost a child. Will glanced round at all the dejected faces and shook his head.

'I'm sorry. We did our best but sometimes it
isn't enough.'

Nobody said anything as they got the child
ready to be taken to the chapel so that her parents could see her. Will left Theatre and tossed
his soiled gown into the basket then went
through to the changing-room to shower. It was
his responsibility to tell the parents the sad
news and it was a job he always hated and
would never get used to.

Little Tara's parents were in the waiting-
room and the minute he went in he saw the fear
in their eyes. He sat them down and gently explained that Tara's injuries had been too severe
to save her. They both cried and he sat with
them for a long time, reassuring them that she
wouldn't have suffered even though he had no
idea whether it was true. But people could only
take so much and he wouldn't add to their pain
when it wouldn't alter the outcome.

It was almost four by the time he left the
hospital and the roads were empty, a thin layer
of frost making the asphalt sparkle in his head-

lights as he drove home. He drew up outside the flat and let his head drop wearily onto the steering-wheel while he tried to summon enough energy to get out of the car. He felt a hundred years old, so tired that his bone-marrow ached, but in the end he managed to open the car door and stumble up the steps to let himself in.

He crept into the flat, cursing softly when he banged his shin on the table by the door. The whole place was in darkness and the air felt wonderfully warm and welcoming after the cold, lonely drive home.

He made his way along the hall, pausing when he came level with Lisa's bedroom. The door was closed and he couldn't hear any sound coming from inside the room yet he knew she was in there, sleeping. He could sense her presence and a pain so sweet and sharp hit him that he had to swallow a groan. He didn't need to see her to know she was there. He didn't need to touch her or speak to her, he just knew. Whenever she was about he sensed it.

Funny how he had never given any thought to it before tonight, but before tonight he hadn't had to think about what he would soon be losing. If Lisa married Cameron then she would no longer be in the flat when he came home. He wouldn't be able to stand in the doorway and simply feel her presence.

A wave of panic suddenly hit him. He didn't know how he was going to carry on living without her, yet at the same time he didn't know how he could stop her leaving. Whichever way he turned, someone would get hurt, and if it came to a choice then it had to be him.

So long as Lisa was happy, nothing else mattered.

Lisa had to drag herself out of bed when the alarm went off shortly before five the following morning. The late night combined with everything else that had happened had left her feeling drained. She stumbled into the bathroom, hoping that a shower would wash away some of her lethargy.

She towelled herself dry then put on Will's old robe because it just happened to be hanging behind the bathroom door. It was miles too big for her but she'd worn it so many times in the past that she barely registered the fact. Rolling up the sleeves the necessary dozen or so turns, she headed for the kitchen in the hope that a mug of coffee would wake up the bits the shower had missed.

Five minutes later, a mug of coffee clutched in her hand, she went into the sitting room and stopped dead at the sight that met her. Will was sprawled out on the sofa, fast asleep. He had taken off his shoes and tie but that was all. He was snoring gently and Lisa felt the oddest sensation start to bubble in the pit of her stomach as she watched his lips rhythmically pucker and relax. It looked for all the world as though he was inviting her to kiss him, and the thought sent her mind into a spin. All of a sudden she found herself transported back to those moments in the car park the night before…

'Humph…what time is it?'

She started so violently when he spoke that a wave of coffee slopped over the side of the mug. She let out a gasp of pain when the scalding droplets spattered her bare feet.

Will immediately swung his legs off the couch. 'Stay there while I get some cold water…'

'Don't fuss! It was only a few drops of coffee. I'll live.'

Lisa wasn't sure why she felt so annoyed all of a sudden. Will was only doing what he always did, trying to take care of her. But for some reason it irritated her that he apparently viewed her as some sort of pathetic creature who couldn't look after herself.

'Whatever you say,' he muttered, sinking back onto the couch and closing his eyes again.

Lisa chewed her lip, wondering why she felt equally annoyed because he had taken her at her word. She couldn't have it both ways. She either wanted him to look after her or she didn't. And yet the choice no longer seemed quite so clear-cut. Why did she suddenly find herself wishing that Will would see her not only as someone whom he wanted to take care of, but as a woman who had a lot to offer him as well?

'Any chance I could have some of that coffee?' he murmured, his eyes opening the barest slit.

'Of course.' She quickly passed him the mug, watching while he took a couple of needy glugs.

'That's better.' He opened his eyes fully this time and grinned as he handed back the mug. All of a sudden everything was back to normal again.

Lisa heaved a heartfelt sigh of relief. Of course she didn't want things to change! She wanted Will to carry on treating her the way he had always done. Why wish to change things when everything was fine the way it was?

'My brain has just about caught up with the rest of me now,' he declared.

'You and your morning coffee,' she teased, squeezing onto the couch beside him. He was still sprawled across the cushions and there wasn't much room. She felt a little spasm shoot through her when her hip rubbed against his, but steadfastly ignored it. She didn't intend to let anything rock the status quo again.

'I don't know why you can't arrange to have it served to you intravenously. That way you could get your morning fix of caffeine before you wake up.'

'Can I help it if I need a little help to get me going of a morning?' he protested mournfully. 'Anyhow, you don't look all that bright-eyed and bushy-tailed this morning, if you don't mind my saying so.'

'I don't feel it, but that's another story and I really don't have the time to bore you with it right now.'

She took a quick swallow of coffee, not wanting to go into the ins and outs of why she looked so tired. Maybe it was silly, but she couldn't face the thought of discussing James and his proposal at that moment. She needed to put a little more distance between herself and what had happened in the car park first. Once she'd got that safely sorted out in her head then she could deal with the rest.

'Anyway, I'd better get a move on or I'll be late for work. Do you want the rest of this?' She handed him the mug then got up and hurried to the door, pausing briefly to glance back. 'What time did you get in, by the way?'

'Just after four.'

Will took another gulp of coffee and Lisa felt that funny bubbling sensation start up once more as she watched him tip back his head and swallow the drink. He had unbuttoned the neck of his shirt and she had a perfect view of his strong, tanned throat. For some reason she found herself unable to look away as her eyes soaked up every familiar detail, only they no longer seemed quite so familiar all of a sudden.

Why had she never noticed just how firm his jaw was or how sensual his lips were? she wondered incredulously. And how had she ignored the fact that his eyes were the most beautiful shade of blue?

Her stunned gaze raced on, taking stock of thick black lashes, strongly marked brows, a nose with just the hint of a crook in it, mahogany-brown hair. It startled her to realise that Will was a very attractive man because she hadn't been aware of that fact before. Will was Will and whether or not he was good-looking hadn't mattered a jot.

Now Lisa felt her heart miss several beats as she found herself wondering if the discovery would affect the way she thought about him in the future. She sincerely hoped not, but deep down she sensed that already something had changed. Realising that Will wasn't just her best friend but an extremely attractive and personable man as well had altered the equation. It was no longer her plus Will equalled friendship. Adding his appeal had added a whole new dimension.

Quite frankly, the idea terrified her but the last thing she wanted was for Will to guess anything was wrong. 'I didn't think you'd be that late getting back,' she said quickly, hoping that he wouldn't notice the quaver in her voice.

'What happened about the little girl you operated on?'

'She died.' He shrugged but she could tell
that he was upset. 'I knew there wasn't much
chance of saving her from the outset. We did
what we could, but it just wasn't enough in the
end.'

'It wasn't your fault, Will,' she protested.

She came back and sat on the arm of the sofa,
putting aside her own problems because she
couldn't bear to see him looking so dejected.
'You mustn't blame yourself when you did everything possible.'

'It's hard not to. You should have seen how
upset the parents were.' He sighed. 'It must be
a nightmare when something like that happens,
Lisa. I don't know how people cope. I'm not
sure I could if it was my child.'

Lisa felt her heart lurch because the thought
of Will's child had instantly conjured up an im-
age of a small boy with tousled brown hair and
a huge grin.

'You'd manage, Will,' she said softly, wondering what had come over her. She loved children and hoped to have some of her own one
day, but she couldn't understand why the
thought of Will's child should have awoken all

her maternal instincts. It was an effort to dismiss the thought but Will needed her support.

'I know how upset the parents must have been, but most people come to terms with their loss eventually. You know that as well as I do,' she said gently.

'S'pose so.' He summoned a sad little smile. 'I know I shouldn't let it get to me like this, but it's hard not to. There can't be anything worse than losing a child. It doesn't bear thinking about.'

'It doesn't,' she agreed, her heart filling with tenderness because it was so typical of Will to feel this way. It was one of the reasons why he was such a wonderful doctor—he cared so deeply about the children he treated and their families. All of a sudden it struck her how much she admired him and it was yet another revelation coming on top of all the others she'd had that morning.

'It must help to get you through a situation like that if you have someone to turn to, like I had you when Gareth died.' She summoned a smile but it was unsettling to have to keep readjusting her view of him. 'I would never have coped half as well if you hadn't been here for me, Will.'

'And very soon you'll have Cameron to turn to, won't you?' He lifted the mug to his lips and drank some more coffee then shrugged. 'You won't need me then, Lisa.'

Of course I will! she wanted to shout, only she couldn't do that. How could she lay any more of a burden on him than she had put on him already? Wasn't it time that she thought about his needs? Will had spoken about having children so he must have been thinking about it. Maybe he had met someone and that was what had triggered such thoughts?

The idea took her breath away. She had been so wrapped up in her own affairs since James had arrived on the scene that she had no idea if Will was seeing someone. Was he? Did that help to explain that comment about her no longer needing him if she married James? Had it been wishful thinking on his behalf because it would leave him free to concentrate on his own relationship?

It all seemed to fit and yet she couldn't describe how it made her feel to think about him and this unknown woman, didn't really want to have to think about it at all. It made her feel all churned up to imagine him falling in love with a woman.

Lisa rose swiftly to her feet, terrified that he would guess she was upset. Not that she had any right to be because Will was entitled to a private life. She should be glad if he had found someone to share his life, but she couldn't deny that the thought of him and another woman made her heart ache in the strangest way.

'I'd better run. I take it that you won't be coming into work this morning after your late night?' she said, hurrying to the door before she gave herself away. How would Will feel if he knew how selfish she was being when he had given up so much to take care of her.

'I wish!' He grimaced. 'I've a list as long as my arm and there is no way I can cancel any of the ops. Most of the kids have been waiting months to have surgery as it is.'

'Can't Ray Maxwell take over for you?' she suggested, thinking how unfair it was that he should have to put in a full day's work on top of the late night. 'I thought the whole reason for taking him on was to lighten your work-load.'

'It will probably pan out like that in the end, but he's still finding his feet. It wouldn't be fair to drop him in at the deep end.'

He stood up and groaned. 'Remind me never to doze off on the sofa again, will you? I feel as though a herd of elephants has trampled all over me.'

'Go and have a shower then you'll feel better,' she advised as he staggered across the room. 'Better still, why don't you try and snatch another couple of hours' sleep? You don't need to be in work till nine, do you?'

'No, I don't. Good idea. That's what I'll do. I'll go and have a power nap, as all the top executives call it.' He grinned when she rolled her eyes. 'You can mock all you like, but I'll be the one tucked up all snug and warm in my bed while you're waiting in the cold to catch your bus.'

'Sadist!' she accused, but he only laughed.

Lisa went to get ready as he disappeared into his room. She slid into fresh underwear then chose a white blouse and tailored grey skirt to wear with it. She pinned her hair into its customary chignon and applied a little make-up and that was it. It had taken her a bare ten minutes to get ready but as she passed Will's room she could hear definite sounds of snoring coming from inside.

Lisa smiled as she left the flat and walked towards the bus stop. Knowing Will, he would be back to his normal self when she next saw him, ready to face whatever problems the day threw at him. It made her see just how strong he was because coping with the kind of workload he undertook on a daily basis would have been far too much for most people.

That was why they'd had such difficulty finding another paediatric surgeon to fill the new post at Dalverston General. Budget cuts meant that staffing levels had been drastically reduced, which in turn put extra pressure on the people who worked there. In fact, several applicants had turned down the job once they had discovered what it entailed.

Will worked cripplingly long hours and thought nothing of doing a full day's work and then being on call at night as well. He was too dedicated to refuse to attend when there was an emergency involving a child, even though the general surgical staff were supposed to cover for him.

He gave one hundred per cent commitment to his work, just as he had given one hundred per cent effort to getting Lisa back on her feet after Gareth had died. Maybe it would be a relief for him to be able to shed part of his burden at last?

Lisa sighed as she put out her hand and signalled for the bus to stop. She hated to think that Will would be better off without her, but the truth had to be faced. She needed to set Will free from his obligation because it wasn't fair to carry on taking up so much of his time.

Marrying James would be the perfect solution and she would think seriously about the idea. Maybe she wasn't head over heels in love with him but she liked him and they got on well together so surely that was enough?

But no matter what happened she would have to make some changes because it was time that she struck out on her own and let Will live his own life. Knowing that he was happy would be some compensation for the fact that she was going to miss him dreadfully.

'We'll increase the antibiotics. We'll also need another set of cultures done so that we can pinpoint exactly which bacteria are causing the trouble.'

Will waited patiently while Lisa finished examining Daniel Kennedy, the eight-year-old who had fallen onto the iron railings. He had phoned the intensive care unit during his break and asked for an update on the child's status. Sister Matthews had informed him that there were definite signs of infection setting in, which was why Will had decided to pop down to see him.

It was what he had feared would happen because a wound like that left the body open to many different kinds of infection. Then there was the problem of the child's large intestine having been damaged, allowing its contents to spill into the boy's abdominal cavity. He knew that it would need a careful balance of antibiotic treatment to pull the boy through, but also knew that if anyone could achieve it, Lisa would. She never gave up if there was a chance she could help a child to get better.

A feeling of warmth ran through his veins so that it was an effort to act casually when she turned. Will saw a wash of colour run up her face when she saw him and the heat in his veins seemed to double in intensity even though he did his best to cool it down.

Lisa is just surprised to see me, he told himself sternly. But he couldn't shake off the feeling that she seemed to be aware of him in a way that she had never been before.

'I thought I'd call in to see how young Daniel is doing,' he explained, not wanting to go any further down that route. Letting himself get hung up on thoughts like that wouldn't help a jot. Lisa was only interested in James. She viewed *him* strictly as a friend. Nevertheless, it was harder than it should have been to dismiss the idea.

'Unfortunately, there seems to be a rapid spread of infection.'

She sighed as she glanced at the clipboard she was holding. Will could see that it held the observations that had been taken since the time Daniel had been admitted to the unit. The careful recording of vital signs—temperature, blood pressure, heart and respiratory rates—was essential in a case like this.

'I was hoping that we might be able to contain it, but it's no longer localised.'

'Not surprising when you consider the type of injury he sustained,' Will said, following her down the ward. 'Infection was almost bound to set in because of the damage to the large intestine. The fact that it took so long to get Daniel into Theatre meant that the bacteria and digestive juices that had escaped into his abdominal cavity had plenty of time to cause havoc.'

'Exactly. And then there's all the other micro-organisms that were introduced via the metal spike. Heaven knows what kind of a cocktail of nasties there is bubbling away inside him.'

She shook her head as she studied the child's notes. 'General antibiotic treatment is hopeless in a case like this. We need to know what we're dealing with. I've asked for another set of cultures so, hopefully, we'll have a better idea once we get the lab results back.'

'When is Leo due back?' he asked, following her into the ward kitchen. 'I've lost track of how long he's been away this time.'

Leo Harrison was the consultant in charge of the paediatric intensive care unit and Lisa's boss. Although Will accepted that Leo was excellent at his job, he disagreed with the fact that the man took so much time off. Leo was much in demand on the lecture circuit and had spent several months that year lecturing on paediatric intensive care regimes.

'After Christmas now, apparently.'

Lisa shrugged as she dropped the clipboard onto the table and went to pour them both a cup of coffee from the pot bubbling away on the hot plate. 'He was supposed to be back next week, but there was a note in my pigeonhole this morning to say that he has decided to take a week's holiday tagged onto the end of his current tour. Evidently, he's spending Christmas in Boston with friends.'

'Nice for some, but it does rather leave you in the lurch.' Will frowned as he accepted the cup of coffee. 'It means there's just you and Sanjay to keep everything ticking over here, plus the new houseman.'

'We'll manage,' she assured him. 'We'll have to.'

'But it still isn't right that you should have all that extra work put on you,' he protested, then looked up when she laughed. 'What's so funny?'

'What about you, Will? When you accepted the consultancy you were told that you would have a team of three paediatric registrars working with you, and so far you've got one. Your workload is far bigger than mine.'

'Maybe, but that doesn't mean it's fair for Leo to go swanning off all the time. I've a good mind to have a word with Roger Hopkins about it. After all, I have a vested interest in this department, bearing in mind so many of my patients end up here.'

'Roger must have given permission for Leo to take the time off,' she pointed out. 'He is the hospital's manager, after all.'

'Then maybe Roger should think about hiring a locum to tide you over. It might be an idea if I suggested it to him.'

'Will, this isn't your problem! I know how you love to play Mr Fix-It, but you can't solve all the problems in the world.'

'I wasn't trying to,' he said shortly, unaccountably hurt by the accusation. Didn't Lisa understand that he was worried about her?

'No, I know. And it was unfair of me to say that.' She took a deep breath and he wondered why he had a horrible feeling that she was about to tell him something he wasn't going to like.

'You were trying to help me and I appreciate it, Will, really I do.'

'But?'

He summoned a smile but his heart was pounding so hard that he felt physically sick. 'There was a definite *but* tagged on there, Lisa, so out with it.'

'*But* you can't spend all your time worrying about me. You have your own life to think about and it's about time I let you get on with it. That's why I've decided it would be better if I moved out of the flat.'

CHAPTER FOUR

LISA bit her lip when she saw the shock on Will's face. It made her feel dreadful to know that he hadn't been expecting her to make that announcement.

Just for a moment she found herself wondering if she should tell him that she hadn't meant it, but what would be the point? She had decided that morning it was time she took charge of her own life and left him free to get on with his. Maybe this was the perfect way to set things in motion.

'So when were you planning on moving?'

She shot him a careful look when she heard how strained he sounded. Was Will annoyed because she had dropped this on him without any warning? She hurried to explain, not wanting him to think that she had been making plans behind his back.

'I've no idea yet. I only decided this morning that it was time I made the effort to find a place of my own.'

'Is there any particular reason for it?' He shrugged when she looked blankly at him. 'I'm not trying to pry, Lisa, but if I've done something to upset you then I would far rather you told me.'

'You haven't done anything, Will! You've been kindness itself and I couldn't be more grateful. I just feel that it's time we each had a bit more space to get on with our lives.'

'Oh, I see.' He gave her a thin smile. 'It can't be easy, having me around all the time when you have James to consider. Sorry for being so dim, Lisa. I should have realised that you needed your privacy.'

'Privacy,' she repeated, then blushed when it hit her what he meant. Will thought that she wanted to find a place of her own so that she could invite James to stay overnight with her, but that couldn't have been further from the truth.

'No, you've got it all wrong…' she began, then broke off when Angela Matthews stuck her head round the door.

'Sorry to interrupt but there's a call for Will in the office. A and E want you to have a look at a three-year-old who's been involved in an RTA, Will.'

'Thanks, Angela. Tell them I'll be right there, will you?'

Will put down his mug as Angela left and smiled at Lisa. 'Looks like I'll have to cut and run. But if you need any help flat-hunting, promise you'll tell me, although I expect Cameron will be keen to give you a hand.'

'I expect so,' she said quietly, her head whirling from the speed by which everything seemed to be happening.

Will hurried away and Lisa sat down at the table to drink her coffee but after a few sips she pushed the cup away. She couldn't help feeling a little hurt by the fact that he hadn't tried to persuade her to stay on at the flat. It made her wonder if he had been simply waiting for her to make the move and that thought was even more upsetting. It was one thing to wonder if she had become a burden to him and another to have proof that it was true.

She had grown used to relying on him but from this point on she had to stand on her own two feet. She was perfectly capable of doing so, of course, but she couldn't deny that not having Will to turn to was going to leave a big gap in her life. The scariest thing of all was wondering if anyone else would ever be able to fill it.

The morning flew past with all the usual traumas and triumphs that dealing with seriously ill children always entailed. Will's RTA case was sent up just before lunch, so Lisa left Angela to get the little girl settled and took the parents into the relatives' room. The young couple were obviously in a state of shock because of what had happened, not helped by the fact that they had both been injured in the accident as well.

'I'm Lisa Bennett, the junior registrar on the IC unit,' she explained as they all sat down. 'I'll be in charge of Chloë's care while she is with us.'

'What about that doctor we saw before—Mr Saunders, I think he said his name was? Won't he be looking after her?'

'Mr Saunders is the surgeon who operated on your daughter. Now that he has finished his part in the proceedings, Chloë will be cared for by staff from this unit.'

Lisa smiled reassuringly at Mandy Trent, the child's mother. 'Mr Saunders will still be involved, of course. In fact, he will be up later to see how Chloë is getting on so if you have any questions about her surgery then he will be happy to explain everything to you.'

'I see. I've no idea how everything works, you understand.' Mandy gave her a wobbly smile. She had a huge bruise on the left side of her face and her left arm was in plaster.

'I've never been in a hospital before and neither has Alan,' she added, referring to the young man sitting beside her. His right arm was in a sling and Lisa could see that his forehead had been stitched as well. It was obvious that the accident had taken its toll on the whole family.

'I'm sure it all seems very confusing at the moment, but you mustn't worry,' Lisa said gently. 'We all want to help Chloë and that's the main thing.'

'How soon will we know if she's going to get better?' Alan put in. 'Mr Saunders told us that he'd had to operate to ease the pressure on her brain and that's serious, isn't it?'

'It is. Chloë sustained a very bad head injury in the crash,' she explained gently. 'Her skull was fractured and Mr Saunders had to remove the pieces of bone then drain away a rather large blood clot that had formed.'

'Does it mean that she'll be...*disabled*?' Mandy pressed a tissue to her mouth to stifle a sob. 'I've read about things like that in magazines, about how kiddies have been left like vegetables after they've hurt their heads.'

'It's impossible to say at this stage if the injury will have caused any lasting damage,' Lisa explained, knowing that it would be wrong to lie to them. 'However, the fact that Chloë received treatment so quickly will have gone in her favour, and Mr Saunders is a highly skilled paediatric surgeon who has performed this type of operation very successfully many times before.'

'But there's no guarantee that she'll not have brain damage,' Alan said bluntly. 'That's what you're really saying, isn't it, Dr Bennett?'

'I think it's best not to look too far ahead at this stage,' she said firmly. 'At the moment our main concern is stabilising Chloë and making sure that her condition doesn't deteriorate. The fact that she has come through the operation is a very positive sign so let's hold onto that.'

She stood up, knowing that no amount of reassurances would lessen the parents' fears for their daughter. 'Why don't you sit with Chloë for a little while? Don't worry about all the tubes and equipment she's attached to. It's there simply to tell us what is going on.'

She escorted the parents back into the IC unit and handed them over to Angela. It was lunchtime by then so she had a word with one of the nurses and told her to page her if she was needed.

The shortage of staff meant that she and Sanjay Kapur, the senior registrar, were having to work twelve-hour shifts at the moment. She would work until six that evening when Sanjay would come on duty and he would work through until six the following morning. Their young houseman, Ben Carlisle, was working from eleven in the morning to eleven at night so his hours overlapped with theirs.

There was no doubt that they were in desperate need of more staff because the workload was taxing. There were never enough free beds on any paediatric IC unit and Dalverston General's unit was no exception. As soon as one child was well enough to be transferred to a ward, another would arrive so there was never any let-up from the pressure.

However, Lisa loved her job and knew that she wouldn't wish to change it. Knowing how vital her role was made up for the long hours she worked, although if she did marry James she might have to think again about her choice of career. Would James be happy with a wife who spent so much of her time away from home?

It was a worrying thought but she decided not to think about it until she had made her decision about James's proposal. She took the lift to the sixth floor where the newly refurbished staff canteen was now sited. The day's menu was chalked up on a board by the door so she paused to study it. The canteen food had improved tremendously since the refurbishment had been carried out, thanks mainly to a local chef who had devised some new menus for them. It was hard to decide what she would have that day.

'I'd try the pork casserole if I was you.'

Lisa looked up when she recognised Dave Carson's voice. 'Good, was it?'

'Superb.' He smacked his lips. 'I'm thinking of bringing Jilly here for our wedding anniversary. Why pay top prices at some snooty restaurant when you can dine here for a fraction of the price?'

'Cheapskate!' she accused him.

'*Moi?*' He tried to look hurt. 'Just because I'm careful with my hard-earned cash doesn't mean I'm being mean. We don't all earn the sort of money that allows us to wine and dine our loved ones at The Blossoms.'

Lisa rolled her eyes. 'I see the grapevine is working well as usual. Who told you I'd been to The Blossoms? Was it Will?'

'No. Mark Dawson popped in to book a table for him and Laura, and happened to see you there last night. Will never mentioned it, but I suppose he's got more important things on his mind at the moment.'

'He has?' Lisa's brows rose questioningly.

'Uh-huh.' Dave moved out of the way as several more members of staff arrived for lunch. He waited until they had gone inside the canteen before continuing. 'So who is she, then, Lisa? You must have an idea.'

'I don't know what you're talking about.'

'This woman Will's seeing, of course. He's obviously got it bad, because he was in a right state last night. Madge and I were tickled pink, to be honest. I don't think either of us thought we'd see the day when a woman got to poor old Will like this one has. So, come on, out with it, then—tell me who she is so I can tell Madge.'

'I've no idea.' It was hard to speak when her heart felt as though it had leapt right into her throat. She shook her head when Dave laughed. 'No, honestly. If Will is seeing someone, he hasn't told me about her, I swear.'

'Really? That does surprise me. I'd have thought you would be the first person he told, knowing how close you two are.' Dave shrugged. 'Still, I suppose there are *some* things you don't share even with your best friends.'

He winked at her then headed towards the lift. Lisa took a deep breath but her appetite seemed to have disappeared all of a sudden. She made her way along the corridor and opened the door to the rooftop terrace. It was bitterly cold out there that day, so cold that it took her breath away, but she stood there for some time, thinking about what she had learned.

It seemed that her suspicions about Will having met someone had been correct. It hurt to know that he had chosen not to tell her what had been going on, yet why should he have done? Will was a free agent and he certainly didn't need *her* permission to fall in love.

A mist of tears filmed her eyes but Lisa
blinked them away. Will deserved some happiness after everything he had done for her in
the past few years and she had no right to feel
upset. They could still be friends, of course,
although she was realistic enough to know that
their relationship was bound to change. Now
that Will had this other woman in his life, he
would no longer have the time to worry about
her.

She went back inside and it felt as though
her heart had never felt so heavy as it did at
that moment. Knowing that Will would shower
the other woman with all the kindness and concern that he had shown to her left Lisa feeling
bereft. The truth was that she was going to miss
him such a lot.

It was a long day. As well as the list of children
who needed elective surgery, there were two
further emergency admissions. Will worked
away with his usual dedication but he did so
with a heavy heart.

Knowing that Lisa would be leaving sooner
than he had anticipated had hit him hard, even
though he knew how stupid it was to let it upset
him. She would have left when she married

Cameron so what difference did a few months make? he tried to reason, but it didn't work. He would give anything for a few more days of her company, let alone several months.

It was almost seven before he put the final staple into the last small patient and sent the child off to the recovery bay. Ray Maxwell had been assisting him for the past hour and Will grimaced as they left Theatre together. 'Been quite a day, hasn't it?'

'It has. I didn't realise just how heavy the workload here was going to be.'

Ray sighed as he flexed his shoulders. He was a good-looking man in his early thirties, a couple of years younger than Will was, in fact. His references had been excellent, which was why he had been hired for the job. However, Will had never been able to rid himself of a faint concern about Ray's commitment.

Ray had changed jobs at least a dozen times since qualifying. Although he had explained at his interview that it had taken him some time to find a post where he felt truly happy, Will suspected that he'd had another reason for moving around so much. Ray wouldn't be the first surgeon who had changed jobs because the pressure had become too much for him to cope with.

'Not having second thoughts, I hope?' he said lightly, opening his locker door. He bit back a sigh when he saw how uncomfortable the younger man looked. It was obvious that Ray had been wondering if he'd made the right decision by accepting the post at Dalverston General.

'I have to admit that I'm not a hundred per cent certain that I've chosen the right job,' Ray said. He shrugged when Will looked at him questioningly. 'Maybe you're happy not to have any social life, Will, but I'm not. I'm not one of those people who want to eat, sleep and dream about their work twenty-four hours a day.'

'Sounds as though you might have chosen the wrong profession, not just the wrong post,' he said dryly, trying to hide his dismay. It had taken them months to find anyone suitable to fill the vacancy and, from the sound of it, they might need to start advertising again shortly.

'Surgery is one of the most demanding areas of medicine that you can choose. It's both physically and mentally draining, no matter where you end up working.'

'Tell me about it!' Ray sighed as he took a towel from his locker and draped it around his neck. 'I was saying much the same to a friend of mine only last week. He made no bones about the fact that he thought I was mad to have gone in for surgery.

'He decided to opt out after he'd done a year as a houseman—he couldn't take the long hours and the poor pay. He's working for one of the big pharmaceutical companies now and you wouldn't believe the perks he gets with his job—company car, free medical insurance, five-star accommodation when he travels abroad. It makes me wonder why I'm doing this job, quite honestly.'

'Because you can make a difference to so many people's lives,' Will said flatly. 'That has to count for an awful lot in my view.'

'Even when it comes at the expense of having any sort of personal life?' Ray shook his head. 'Sorry, Will, but I'm just not as dedicated as you. I want to have some fun while I'm still young enough to enjoy myself. I'll be content to sit by the fire with my pipe and slippers quite soon enough!'

Ray laughed as he headed for the shower. Will slowly undressed but he had to admit that

Ray's comments had touched a nerve. Was he
in danger of becoming set in his ways, perhaps?
He rarely went out of a night mainly because
he had so little time to do so. And as for going
out on a date... Well!

He wrapped a towel around his waist and
padded, barefoot, into the shower room.
Turning on the jets, he let the hot water drum
down on his head and shoulders while he
thought about how dull his life had become in
the past few years. It consisted of work and
evenings spent in the flat and, although he had
been quite content up to now, maybe it was
time that he made some changes, especially
now that Lisa would be leaving.

He sighed. Everything seemed to hinge on
that, didn't it? He had been content because
what little free time he'd had in the past few
years he had spent with Lisa. That was why he
hadn't felt the need to go out and socialise.

They would open a bottle of wine and watch
a movie together, maybe go for a pizza, although they hadn't done that for a while now,
not since Cameron had become a permanent
fixture in her life. But now all that was going
to change because Lisa was moving on and
moving out and *he* had to start getting his life

back together, although he wasn't sure exactly where to start.

He frowned as he turned off the water and towelled himself dry. He could invite someone out, maybe one of the nurses from the children's ward. There were a number of unmarried women working there and he was friends with most of them.

Where to take her was a problem. It was so long since he had asked anyone out on a date that he wasn't sure what the form was nowadays. The cinema was always a reliable standby or maybe dinner. There were a number of new restaurants in Dalverston so he could make some enquiries and find out which ones were the best. At least it would be a start.

Only he didn't want to invite anyone to go out with him, did he? He didn't want to start a relationship, knowing that it could never really mean anything to him. It wouldn't be right and it certainly wouldn't be fair.

Will took a deep breath but the ache in his heart wouldn't budge. The plain truth was that if he couldn't have Lisa then he didn't want anyone at all.

*   *   *

Lisa had been delayed because Daniel Kennedy had taken a sudden turn for the worse shortly before she'd been due to go off duty. It was obvious that the infection was spreading and that the increased dosage of antibiotics wasn't working.

Daniel's medical notes, which his GP had forwarded to them, showed that the boy had received several prescriptions for different antibiotic drugs in the past year. Unfortunately, that had increased the possibility that the child had built up a resistance to some of the more commonly prescribed antibiotics, making them ineffective in this instance.

Lisa phoned the lab but, as she had feared, the cultures wouldn't be ready for another twenty-four hours. It left her with no option but to try another broad-spectrum antibiotic even though she hated the feeling that she was batting in the dark. Until the lab identified which type of bacteria they were dealing with, she wouldn't be able to tailor the treatment to combat it.

She wrote Daniel up for the new drugs then explained to his parents what she was doing and why it was necessary. Like so many people, Mr and Mrs Kennedy had had no idea that different bacteria required different antibiotic treatment so it all took some time. However, Lisa didn't resent spending the time explaining it to the couple. It would help if they understood why Daniel hadn't been responding as they had hoped. Once he was started on the right treatment then she was hopeful that his condition would rapidly improve.

She left the IC unit at last and went to the staffroom to collect her coat. Angela Matthews was going off duty as well so they rode down in the lift together. They were just crossing the foyer when Lisa spotted Will hurrying back into the building.

'Don't tell me you're still here,' she said, frowning. 'I thought you would have left ages ago.'

'I wish!' he declared.

'No rest for the wicked, eh?' Angela teased.

'Well, I must have been *really* bad somewhere along the line,' he retorted, grinning at her.

Lisa felt a little flash of awareness light up inside her when he included her in the smile. Once again she was struck by how very attractive he was, especially when he smiled like that.

She couldn't believe that she had never noticed it before that morning.

Why had she been so completely unaware of his charms before? she found herself wondering, but there was no easy way to explain it. However, it was worrying to realise how much the situation had changed in a few short hours so that it was an effort to compose her features into a suitable expression when Will turned to her after Angela had hurried away.

'I was driving out of the gates when I had a call to say that one of the kids I operated on the other day had fallen over on his way to the bathroom and done himself some damage. Good job I hadn't made it all the way home, wasn't it?'

'I suppose so, but you really can't keep on this way, Will,' she said worriedly. 'You need to take some time off or you'll run yourself into the ground.'

'I'm off over Christmas so I'll get a break then. I'll probably sleep for the whole holiday!'

'Aren't you going to your parents' for Christmas?' she asked in surprise because she had assumed that was what he would do. She'd been invited to go with him several times since she had been living at the flat and had always enjoyed herself. Will's family were as easy-going as he was and always made her feel very welcome.

Her own parents had divorced when she was a small child so Christmases had been very quiet affairs while she'd been growing up. There had been just her and her mother to celebrate the day but they had always tried to make it special, even though there had only been the two of them.

She had missed her mother dreadfully after Helen Bennett had died so tragically of a heart attack while Lisa had been in her third year at med school. Fortunately she had been seeing Gareth at the time and he had helped her through that very difficult period. Will had also been wonderfully supportive, lending her a shoulder to cry on whenever Gareth hadn't been around. She didn't know how she would have coped without them both.

'Not this year, I'm afraid. Mum and Dad have decided to go away for Christmas for a change. Simon and Diane asked me if I'd like to go to them, but it's a bit of a drag, driving all the way to Devon for a couple of days, so I decided not to bother.'

'I see.' Lisa sighed because the thought of him spending Christmas on his own made her feel awful. Even when they had both been working, they had at least managed to have lunch together in the canteen. It would be odd not to spend any time with Will that Christmas.

'I could ask James if he would mind if you came to the cottage,' she suggested, thinking fast.

'It's kind of you, Lisa, but I really don't think it would be a good idea.'

'I'm sure he wouldn't mind, Will,' she insisted, wondering what had put that edge in his voice.

'Lisa, the last thing that Cameron wants is me hanging around.' He gave her a crooked smile. 'I'd feel exactly the same in his shoes, too. Remember that old saying about two's company and three is a crowd? Anyway, I've already made plans so you don't need to worry about me.'

'You have?' she said uncertainly, wondering if he was telling her the truth.

'Uh-huh.' He tapped the side of his nose and winked at her. 'I have something lined up, shall we say?'

'Oh, I see.' All of a sudden Lisa realised how foolish she was. Of course Will wasn't going to be on his own this Christmas! He was probably looking forward to having the flat all to himself so that he could invite his girlfriend round for the day.

Or the night, a small voice whispered.

The thought of him spending the night with some woman made her feel so sick all of a sudden that it was an effort to pretend everything was fine. 'Well, that's OK, then. As long as I know that you won't be on your own, I can go off and enjoy myself with a clear conscience.'

'I shall be fine,' he said firmly. 'And now I'd better get upstairs and see what's happened. Fingers crossed that it doesn't take too long to sort it all out.'

Lisa watched him hurrying towards the lifts then quickly left the building. It had started to rain but she barely noticed it as she made her way to the bus stop. She couldn't seem to rid herself of the pictures that were filling her head, pictures of Will making love to some faceless woman.

It shocked her that she should be having thoughts like that because it had never happened before. She had never *once* thought about

Will in that context. It made her wonder what was wrong with her now and why she found the idea of him and this woman so difficult to deal with. Surely she couldn't be jealous?

Her breath caught because she didn't want to believe it was true, but how else could she explain the way she was feeling? Thinking about Will making love to another woman made her feel as though the bottom had dropped out of her world. It also made her see how impossible it would be to carry on living at the flat. It was bad enough imagining them together but how would she feel if Will invited his girlfriend to stay one night while she was there?

She would have to make a concerted effort to find somewhere else to live as soon as she could, although it was doubtful whether she could find anywhere before Christmas. But once Christmas was over, she would definitely move out of the flat.

Lisa sighed. She would have to move if she accepted James's proposal, but that didn't make her feel any better about the idea. Leaving Will was going to be very hard and it didn't make a scrap of difference what her reasons were for doing so.

CHAPTER FIVE

IT DIDN'T take Will long to work out what was the problem with his patient. Twelve-year-old Andrew Brown had been suffering from displacement of the upper epiphysis—the growing end of the femur. Because the bone was still growing, the epiphysis was separated from the shaft of the femur by a plate of cartilage, leaving an area of weakness that was susceptible to injury. When Andrew had fallen off a climbing frame during a school PE lesson a few weeks earlier, the epiphysis had slipped out of position.

Will had manipulated the displaced parts of the bone back into position and fixed them with metal pins. Unfortunately, Andrew had slipped in the bathroom that evening and wrenched the pins free. Will would now have to redo the operation, much to the boy's dismay.

'I'm sorry, son, but there really is no choice. If I don't realign the sections of your femur again, you'll carry on limping.'

'But that means I'll have to stay in hospital.' Andrew was doing his best not to cry. 'It's Christmas soon, Mr Saunders!'

'I know and it's really tough luck, but there really isn't any alternative.' Will patted the boy's shoulder, thinking how much he would have hated the thought of being stuck in hospital at Christmas when he'd been a child.

'It won't be that bad, Andrew. Honestly. The staff organise all sorts of things at Christmas—games and a party, even a visit from Santa Claus.'

'I'm too old to believe in Father Christmas,' Andrew muttered.

'Really?' Will shrugged. 'Then you won't be wanting the presents he brings for all the children in the ward, will you?'

'Well…' Andrew wavered, obviously not wanting to miss out on any treats.

Will laughed. 'Don't worry. You'll get a present even if you don't believe in Santa any more.' He lowered his voice confidingly. 'Just don't say anything to the little ones, will you? It would be a shame to spoil the fun for them.'

'I won't,' Andrew promised, looking a little happier at being entrusted to keep the secret.

Mr and Mrs Brown arrived just then, looking anxious as they hurried to their son's bed. Rachel Hart, the ward sister, had phoned to tell them about Andrew's accident and they wanted to know how much damage he had done to himself.

Will explained that he would have to redo the operation and that it would entail Andrew being kept in hospital a while longer. They were obviously upset to learn that their son wouldn't be home for Christmas, but they tried not to show it as they cheered him up by telling him what a good time he would have in the hospital.

They were the sort of parents whom Will enjoyed dealing with, full of common sense and wanting only what was best for their child. He left them talking to the boy and made his way from the ward, stopping off on the way to have a word with Rachel and tell her what was happening.

Rachel sighed after he had finished explaining it all. 'I thought as much. As soon as Julie came to tell me that Andrew had fallen over, I feared the worst.'

'How come he was allowed to go to the bathroom on his own?' Will asked, lounging against the door frame as weariness suddenly caught up with him. 'I thought you didn't allow the kids to wander about on their own when they were first on crutches.'

'We don't. Unfortunately, Andrew slipped out when we weren't looking.' Rachel sighed. 'We're short-staffed at the moment and there's only been the two of us on duty all afternoon. Andrew hates being accompanied to the bathroom and took advantage of the fact that we were busy with one of the other children. The end result is you having to redo all your good work, Will. Sorry!'

'These things happen,' he said lightly, knowing it wasn't Rachel's fault. Everyone was working flat out at the present time to make up for the shortage of staff.

'Especially when you're trying to do the work of ten people!' She grinned at him. 'Same old story throughout the hospital. I heard that you'd been called in several nights this week.'

'I don't know why I bother going home, to be honest.' He laughed ruefully. 'I'd be better off camping out in my office—that way I might get a couple of hours' sleep.'

'There is being dedicated and being dedicated,' Rachel retorted. 'Even I have to accept that I need to get away from this place once in a while.'

'I'm sure you're right,' Will agreed. 'Lisa was saying much the same thing earlier, funnily enough. She was trying to persuade me to take some time off,' he explained when Rachel looked at him quizzically.

'She was right, too, because the pressure does start to get to you. You spend most of your time struggling to keep on top of the job so that when you do have any time off then you end up too exhausted to enjoy it. My days off are usually spent sleeping!'

'How would you fancy doing something a bit more exciting for a change?' Will said hesitantly. He hurried on, not wanting to give himself time to think better of what he was doing. Hadn't he decided that he needed to think about his social life so why not take the opportunity to put his plans into action? He liked Rachel and had always got on extremely well with her so what harm could there be in asking her out?

'What do you have in mind?' she asked, grinning at him. 'I warn you that I'm not into extreme sports so hang-gliding is out and so is bungee-jumping!'

'And here I was thinking that you were a woman who loved taking risks.' He laughed when Rachel rolled her eyes. 'OK, then, how about the cinema one evening? That should be nice and safe. It's been ages since I saw a film and it would be great if you would come with me.'

'I'd love to, Will, so long as I'm not stepping on any toes.'

'Sorry?'

'You and Lisa.' She shrugged when he looked blankly at her. 'I've never been exactly sure what the situation is regarding you two.'

'We're just friends,' he assured her, although the words almost stuck in his throat. Maybe it was foolish to long to be more than Lisa's friend but he couldn't help it, just as he couldn't ignore the truth. Lisa regarded *him* as her best friend. Period. She certainly didn't imagine them having any other kind of a relationship.

'In that case, I'd love to come to the cinema with you, Will. Now all we have to decide is when, and *that* could be the really tricky bit. Do you think we're really going to be able to get some time off together?'

'I'll wangle it somehow. So, when are you next off duty of an evening?' he said, quashing any reservations he had. He was only asking Rachel out on a date so why get all het up about it?

'Tomorrow, as it happens. I've got the whole day off and—barring flood, fire and pestilence breaking out in Dalverston—I fully intend not to set foot inside this place. We could go tomorrow night, if you're free?'

'I'll make sure I am.' Will smiled, not wanting Rachel to guess how unsure he was about this. He could tell himself a dozen times that he wasn't doing anything wrong but he couldn't help feeling worried.

'I'm not sure what time the evening performance starts at the Ritz so I'll check it out and phone you at home, if that's all right with you? We could go for a pizza after the film if you like.'

'Fine,' she agreed, then looked round when Andrew's parents appeared to have a word with her.

Will bade them all goodbye and left, but the whole time he was riding down in the lift he kept wondering if he had done the right thing. He liked Rachel and he wouldn't want her to think that he was using her. He also wouldn't like to upset Lisa…

He sighed when it struck him how ridiculous that idea was. Why should Lisa care because he had asked Rachel out? Lisa had her own future to think about and plan for. He may as well face the fact that he didn't feature in it.

It was almost lunchtime next day before Daniel Kennedy's lab results came back. Lisa took the printout into the office and sat down at the desk to read it. She'd been having trouble concentrating all morning, mainly because Will had behaved so strangely the night before.

It had been almost nine before he had arrived home and he had been unusually quiet for the rest of the evening. Lisa had gone to bed at half past ten, but he had stayed up, watching television. She had got up in the early hours of the morning for a drink of water and been surprised when she had realised the television had still been switched on.

She had no idea what time Will had finally gone to bed but it must have been very late. She'd left for work before he had got up so she hadn't spoken to him yet that day. However, she couldn't shake off the feeling that he had something on his mind.

Had it anything to do with this woman he was seeing?

She sighed as she picked up the lab report. It was no business of hers what was going on, as he had made it abundantly clear. He certainly hadn't confided in her about his feelings for this woman, whoever she was. Will obviously wanted to keep their relationship private and she had to respect that.

Lisa quickly read through the lab report, feeling her heart sink when she discovered that the bacterium had been identified as a strain of methicillin-resistant *Staphylococcus aureus*, or MRSA as it was commonly called. It was a serious infection which could cause many dangerous complications such as endocarditis—inflammation of the lining of the heart—and bone, liver and lung infection.

As its name implied, this particular type of bacterium was resistant to methicillin, one of the most frequently used antibiotics, and it could cause havoc if it spread throughout the IC unit. All the children would need to be tested to see if they had been infected by it and Daniel would need to be isolated. It was going to cause an awful lot of headaches.

Lisa went into the unit and told Angela what had happened. They both agreed that Roger Hopkins would need to be informed because they would be unable to accept any more patients into the unit until they knew just how widespread the infection was. MRSA spread through patient contact, respiratory droplets and food, and it was a major problem in many hospitals throughout the world.

Fortunately, Daniel was infected by a strain that could be treated with vancomycin. Lisa wrote him up for the drugs then explained to his parents about the lab results and why they would need to move Daniel to the isolation room. They were naturally worried and she did her best to reassure them, but it wasn't easy to calm their fears when it would have been wrong to play down the seriousness of the child's condition.

It was almost two before everything was organised. Daniel was safely ensconced in the side room and Angela and Jackie Meredith, the staff nurse on the unit, were busily taking bloods to send to the lab. There were seven children in the unit and each would need to be tested.

The infection control team had arrived and were testing the equipment that was used in the unit for traces of MRSA. The bacterium could inhabit the breathing apparatus and intravenous lines that were used on the children so it was vital that they made sure there were no signs of it. Other members of the team were carrying out tests in the operating theatre where Daniel had had his surgery, which meant that all elective paediatric surgery had been cancelled. Until they could be sure that the bacteria hadn't colonised any of the equipment, only emergency surgery would be performed, and that in one of the other theatres.

The staff canteen was almost empty by the time Lisa arrived for a late lunch. Most of the hot food had gone and she was too hungry to wait until there was any more ready. She put a plate of tuna sandwiches on her tray then added a jam doughnut and a bottle of mineral water and went to the till to pay.

She was just about to go and sit down when Will came in and she saw him hesitate when he spotted her. For a moment she honestly thought he was going to turn right around again and leave, and the thought made her heart suddenly ache. Since when had Will felt it necessary to avoid her?

Will summoned a smile as he let the canteen door slam shut behind him. He knew it was silly but he would have given anything to avoid having to talk to Lisa at that moment. He still wasn't comfortable with the idea of asking Rachel to go out with him, even though there was no reason why he should feel bad about it. It wasn't as though he was letting Lisa down by taking another woman out, for heaven's sake! However, it was hard to dismiss the guilty feelings that assailed him as he went over to speak to her.

'I see you've drawn the short straw for lunch as well,' he said, striving for lightness.

'Looks like it.' She gave him a cool little smile then carried her tray over to a nearby table and sat down with her back towards him.

Will frowned because he had the distinct impression that she had quite deliberately snubbed him. He quickly collected a plate of sandwiches and a cup of tea then went to join her, glancing pointedly at the empty chair.

'Mind if I sit here?'

'That's up to you.'

She ignored him as she started to peel away the film from her sandwiches. Will put his tray on the table and sat down. He shot her a wary look but she didn't even glance at him as she started to eat her lunch. He unwrapped his own sandwiches, wishing that he had some idea what was going on. Lisa was obviously annoyed with him, but what about?

His heart suddenly jolted and he put down the plate with a thud. Had she found out about him asking Rachel out?

The thought that she might be upset about him taking the other woman to the cinema made him feel all churned up inside. He couldn't help wondering why she didn't like the idea. Was it possible that Lisa was jealous, perhaps?

His mind seemed to go into overdrive at that point, thoughts whizzing around so fast in his head that he felt positively giddy. It was far too much of an effort to pretend there was nothing wrong.

'Are you annoyed with me, Lisa?' he said hoarsely.

'Why should I be annoyed with you, Will? After all, if you suddenly decide that you don't want to talk to me, that's your business, isn't it?'

The bite in her voice brought him back to earth with a thump and he stared at her in dismay. 'What do you mean?'

'Oh, *please*! Do you think I'm stupid or something?' She tossed her sandwich onto the plate and glared at him. 'It was blatantly obvious that you weren't exactly thrilled to see me in here when you arrived. Given the chance, you would have turned tail and run! I don't know what I'm supposed to have done, Will, but if there is a problem then I would much prefer it if you came right out and said so.'

And he could just imagine her reaction if he did, he thought grimly. How would she react if he told her that the only problem he had at the moment was the thought of her leaving him? A confession like that would naturally lead to more questions, ones he wasn't sure that he could answer. How did he *really* feel about Lisa? He knew it was more than friendship, but was it the sort of all-consuming love that he had always dreamed of finding?

His parents had a wonderfully happy marriage and he had hoped that one day he might follow suit. The problem was he had never imagined that Lisa would be the woman he had been waiting for all these years. The idea was still too new and shocking for him to feel comfortable with it. His role had been that of friend and advisor for so long that it was hard to make the transition, especially when it would cause so many problems. Lisa was on the brink of marrying Cameron so how could he upset all her plans by admitting that he *thought* he was in love with her?

It could mark the end of their friendship because once she realised that his feelings for her were deeper than she had believed them to be then it would make her feel uncomfortable. He could just about live with the thought of her leaving if he knew that he wouldn't lose her friendship as well.

'Mmm, we are touchy today,' he said, grinning at her and praying that she couldn't tell how much it cost him to lie. 'I wasn't trying to avoid you, Lisa. I'd just remembered that I was supposed to give Ray a message. I couldn't decide whether I should go back and find him, or leave it until after I'd had something to eat.'

'Oh! I see.'

It was all Will could do not to grovel when he heard how wretched she sounded. It was obvious that she was giving herself a hard time for having accused him of trying to avoid her, and it made him feel even more guilty. He rushed to reassure her.

'Sorry if I seemed a bit off with you. It wasn't intentional. Good job we know one another so well, isn't it?' He smiled at her and was rewarded when she gave him a tentative smile in return.

'It is. And I'm sorry, too, for being so touchy.' She pulled a piece of crust off her sandwich and sighed. 'It's been one of those mornings, shall we say?'

'Tell me about it,' he said lightly. 'I've had to cancel three ops because of this outbreak of MRSA. The worst thing is that all the children were admitted yesterday so they would be ready to go to Theatre this morning. There's a lot of angry parents wanting to know why this has happened.'

'It's a real problem, isn't it?' she agreed. 'Hopefully, the infection control team will get it sorted out pretty quickly and give us the all-clear.'

'If it's got into any of the equipment then it could take some time,' he warned. 'You know how hard it is to shift the bacterium once it gets a hold.'

'I know. I feel so bad about poor little Daniel Kennedy. He's going to need antibiotic treatment for at least two weeks—probably longer, in fact. MRSA can have a long-term effect so it's quite normal to have a patient on antibiotics for months after they've suffered a severe infection like this.'

'It's one of the biggest problems of having over-prescribed antibiotics in the past,' Will agreed. 'If more care had been taken about how often they were prescribed then the bacterium wouldn't have mutated this way. In Japan there is a strain of *Staph* which is partly resistant to vancomycin. We won't have anything left to treat it with soon.'

'It doesn't bear thinking about. I feel so guilty that I didn't start treating Daniel for it sooner. I just hope that it hasn't spread to any of the other children.'

'Hey, you weren't to know!' He frowned when he saw how dejected she looked. 'Come on, Lisa, you know very well that you did everything you could.'

'Mmm.'

'Never mind "Mmm"! You did and that's the end of it. OK?'

'Yes, sir!' She grinned when he rolled his eyes. 'Not that I'm implying you were pulling rank on me, of course.'

'Heaven forbid!' He shook his head when she laughed. 'Anyway, I wasn't trying to do that so sorry if it came across that way.'

'Apology accepted on one condition.'

'Which is?'

'That you treat me to a lovely soppy video this evening. I feel like doing something to take my mind off work so how about renting that new film that everyone's been talking about?'

She smiled at him and Will felt his heart turn over when he saw the warmth and laughter in her hazel eyes. 'And as an added inducement because I know romantic comedies are not really your thing, I'll treat us to a pizza *and* allow you to choose the toppings. Is it a deal?'

Lisa picked up her cup as she waited for him to answer. Not that she had any doubt he would agree, of course. Even though Will preferred adventure films to comedies he would go along with her choice. He was always so considerate in the way he treated her.

That thought made her frown because it made her see just how considerate he really was. He always let her choose which video they rented and what kind of take-away meals they ordered. He claimed that he didn't mind one way or the other, but all of a sudden she realised he had said that simply because he had wanted her to have what *she'd* wanted. Will always put her first in everything he did.

The thought made her feel all warm and tingly and she abruptly put down her cup. It shocked her to suddenly realise how spoilt she had been in the past few years. No man could have looked after her as well as Will had done. How could James hope to live up to him?

The thought made her mind spin so it was a moment before she realised Will had said something.

'Sorry, I didn't catch that,' she said, hoping that he couldn't tell how disturbed she felt. Maybe she shouldn't measure the two men against each other, but she couldn't help it and there was no doubt at all that Will had come out on top.

'I said that I'm going out tonight, Lisa, so I'll have to take a rain check on your offer of a pizza,' he repeated obligingly.

'Out?' She stared at him in bewilderment because it was the last thing she had expected him to say. She couldn't remember the last time Will had been out of an evening.

'Yes.' He cleared his throat then hurried on. 'I'm taking Rachel to the cinema then we're going for something to eat afterwards.'

'Rachel?' she repeated, struggling to follow what he was saying.

'Rachel Hart—from Children's Medical,' he explained shortly. He picked up his cup then put it down again and sighed. 'Look, I can always cancel if you have your heart set on seeing that video. I'm sure Rachel won't mind if we make it another night.'

'Of course you mustn't cancel your date!' she said quickly. She picked up her cup and made herself drink a little of the tea, but it was an effort to swallow the tepid liquid when her stomach was churning.

Was Rachel the woman whom Will had been seeing? It had been one thing to speculate about some unknown female, but it was quite another to actually have a name and a face to go with it. She knew Rachel and liked her both as a person and as a wonderful nurse, but…

But—what?

What possible objection could she have? Rachel was lovely. Everyone who worked with her said the same thing, that she was one of the nicest people they had ever met. If she'd had to choose someone for Will then Rachel would have been an ideal candidate, in fact. Nevertheless, Lisa couldn't deny that the thought of him and Rachel seeing each other made her feel so queasy that it was an effort to pretend everything was fine.

It was far too much of an effort, in fact, and she hurriedly put down her cup. Pushing back the cuff of her white coat, she made a great show of checking her watch. 'Is that the time? I'll have to run.'

'What about your lunch?' Will said, frowning as he looked at her half-eaten sandwich.

'I'll take it with me.' She quickly rewrapped the sandwich in cling film and shoved it into her coat pocket.

'I've some parents coming to see me and I don't want to keep them waiting,' she ad-libbed.

She hated having to lie to him but the thought of him guessing how devastated she felt was infinitely worse. She should be pleased that Will had found someone as lovely as

Rachel to share his life but she couldn't help feeling as though the bottom had dropped out of her world. It was an effort to summon a smile as she picked up her tray.

'There's going to be enough problems as it is once everyone finds out about Daniel Kennedy.'

'I doubt the infection will have spread to the other kids,' Will assured her. 'You've taken immediate steps to isolate him and the nursing staff on the IC unit are very much aware of the dangers of cross-infection. Angela continually drums it into them and the level of hygiene there couldn't be better.'

'Oh, I know! But the parents are bound to be worried when they find out what has happened,' she said quickly, not wanting him to think that she was criticising the staff in any way.

She edged away from the table, praying that she could hide her feelings for as long as it took to make her escape. Will was seeing Rachel. Would she ever get used to the idea?

'I suppose so. Who's coming to see you?' he asked, biting into his sandwich.

'Oh, um, Chloë Trent's parents,' she fibbed, feeling even worse. She'd never lied to Will before, had never had to because she had always felt that she could tell him anything. It hurt so much to know how everything had changed. 'Anyway, I must dash. I'll catch you later, I expect.'

'I doubt it. I've got a meeting with Roger Hopkins and Morgan Grey to work out what we are going to do if the main paediatric theatre is out of action for any length of time. After that, I'm planning on taking the rest of the day off.' He grinned up at her. 'I shall be a gentleman of leisure this afternoon, so there!'

'Lucky for some!' she retorted, doing her best to respond the way Will would expect her to. 'Think about me slaving away while you're swanning about, won't you?'

'Oh, I shall, Lisa. I shall.'

There was something in his voice when he said that which made her breath catch, but she knew how foolish it would be to imagine it meant anything.

Will had been teasing her, she told herself sternly as she left the canteen. He hadn't been trying to imply that she was never far from his thoughts. They were simply friends—good friends, admittedly, but nothing more than that. He certainly didn't think about her the same way as he thought about Rachel.

Tears welled into her eyes all of a sudden but she dashed them away. She had no right to feel miserable because Will had found happiness at last. She should be pleased for him and for Rachel, too. Everyone needed someone to love them. Will needed Rachel and she needed James.

Her mind stalled on that thought. No matter how hard she tried, she simply couldn't picture the future she and James would have together. All she could think about was that Will wouldn't be there with her to share it, and it seemed wrong.

What kind of a future did she have to look forward to without her dearest friend?

CHAPTER SIX

WILL left the hospital shortly before three after discussing the current crisis with Roger Hopkins, the hospital's manager, and Morgan Grey, the head of surgery.

They had all agreed there was little they could do until the infection control team had finished their investigations, which would probably be the following morning at the earliest. However, the news so far had been very encouraging. It appeared they had found no trace of the MRSA bacterium in any of the equipment they had tested.

It could turn out that Daniel himself was the source of the infection and not the equipment that had been used during his surgery or his subsequent stay in the intensive care unit. Nevertheless, Theatre Three—the dedicated paediatric theatre—was to be given a thorough overhaul by the cleansing department and all the equipment that was used there would be either sterilised or discarded. It was a costly exercise but at least they had the comfort of knowing they were doing all they could to contain the outbreak.

Will drove out of the gates and turned onto the bypass, wondering how to fill in the afternoon. It was such a rare event for him to have any time off during the day that he wasn't sure what to do with it. In the end, he decided to go back to the flat and tidy up then go for a run. It had been ages since he'd had the time to go jogging and the exercise would do him good.

It didn't take him long to tidy up. With both him and Lisa working such long hours they spent very little time at home and, consequently, there wasn't much to do. He vacuumed the sitting room and put some washing into the machine then settled down to read the paper, promising himself that he would go for his run as soon as he had finished it.

He woke up a couple of hours later, feeling decidedly out of sorts for having dozed off in the middle of the day. So much for having time off, he thought ruefully as he got up from the sofa. He'd wasted most of it by sleeping, but at least he still had time for a run. He'd arranged to collect Rachel at seven but there would be plenty of time to shower and change when he got back.

He quickly changed into his running gear and set off. It had been so long since he had done any real physical exercise that he was puffing before he got to the end of the road. He gritted his teeth and carried on, but it was a relief when he arrived back home an hour later. He stripped off his shorts and top and headed for the shower. It had just turned six and he needed to hurry up if he didn't want to be late collecting Rachel.

He quickly showered then dressed, hesitating when it came to a decision about what he should wear. Normally he grabbed the first shirt and tie that came to hand but that night he stood in front of the mirror and tried first one tie then another to see how well they matched.

He sighed because both ties looked much the same to him. If only Lisa were there, he thought wistfully, she could have helped him choose the right one to wear that night for his date.

A searing pain lanced through him and he took a deep breath. What was the point of lying to himself? It was Lisa he really wanted to be taking out on a date, Lisa he wanted in his life tonight and every night to come—nobody else. He could tell himself a million times that he was doing the right thing by getting on with his life but it wouldn't change how he felt. Was it really fair to Rachel to start up a relationship when nothing could ever come of it?

He left the bedroom and strode along the hall, intending to phone Rachel and make some excuse to cancel their arrangement. He was just about to pick up the receiver when the front door opened and Lisa appeared. She stopped dead when she saw him and Will saw the oddest expression cross her face.

He felt a tingling sensation start at his toes and work its way up his body. Why on earth was Lisa staring at him that way?

Lisa felt a numbing pain grip her heart as she looked at Will. She couldn't remember when she had *ever* seen him looking so smart! Her eyes skimmed over the pale grey shirt and toning, darker grey tie he was wearing and the pain steadily grew worse.

He had obviously made an effort that evening and it was the reason why he had gone to so much trouble that hurt so bitterly. Will had wanted to look good for Rachel because her opinion mattered to him. If Lisa had needed proof of how he felt about the other woman, now she had it.

'It doesn't go, does it?'

She jumped when he spoke and raised startled eyes to his face. 'I'm sorry?'

'This tie. It doesn't go with the shirt.' He cast a rueful glance down. 'I'm hopeless at matching things up. I can't seem to tell what goes with what.'

'It's fine, Will, really it is.'

She fixed a smile to her mouth, praying that he couldn't tell how much it had upset her to acknowledge how deep his feelings for Rachel really were. 'I was just thinking how smart you look, actually. I hope Rachel will appreciate the effort you've made for her sake.'

She tried to inject a teasing note into her voice but it wasn't wholly successful and she saw him frown.

'You don't think I've gone over the top, do you? I don't want to give Rachel the wrong idea.'

She frowned when she heard the anxiety in his voice. 'What do you mean exactly by the wrong idea?'

'Well, it's just a night out.' He shrugged but she could tell how uncomfortable he was feeling. 'I wouldn't like Rachel to think I was coming on too strong or anything.'

'Don't be silly!' It was an effort to hold her smile when she saw how worried he looked. It was obvious that he must be deeply attracted to Rachel if he was so concerned about making the right impression.

'Of course Rachel won't think that you're coming on too strong, Will. She'll be flattered that you've made the effort to dress up and that's all.'

'Well, if you say so...' he began.

'I do.' Suddenly Lisa couldn't bear to discuss it any further. She shrugged off her coat and hung it on a peg then started towards the kitchen.

'I'm starving,' she said, deliberately changing the subject. 'I hope there's some food in the fridge. It's been ages since we went shopping.'

'There's some chops in the freezer and there should be some salad left, although I should have checked what we had in this afternoon. Let's have a look and if there's nothing you fancy, I can drive down to the shops and pick up some bits and pieces before I go out.'

Will moved away from the phone at the same moment as she tried to pass him, and they collided. Lisa's breath left her body in a small gasp when she found her breasts crushed against the hard wall of his chest. All she had on was a thin cotton blouse and Will was just wearing a shirt. It felt as though there was nothing separating their bare flesh...

'Sorry! Ladies first.' He stepped aside and bowed but there was a tautness about him that belied his joking tone.

Lisa summoned a smile but her legs felt as though they were stuffed with cotton wool as she led the way down the hall. Had Will felt it, too? she wondered shakily. Felt the sudden flare of sexual awareness which had passed between them? Or was it only she who had felt it, she who had been so aware of him that it had taken every scrap of self-control she possessed not to twine her arms around his neck and draw his head down so that she could kiss him...?

'Yep. There's some salad left, as I thought, plus half a dozen eggs as well if you don't fancy the chops.'

She took a deep breath when Will glanced round because it would be unforgivable to let him guess what she'd been thinking. How would Will feel if he discovered that she was having thoughts like that about him? Would he be shocked, embarrassed or disgusted even? He had been Gareth's best friend as well as hers and he might very well believe that it was wrong of her to harbour such feelings.

'I'll make myself an omelette, then.' It was an effort to keep the ache out of her voice but she did her best. 'I don't think I can be bothered to wait for the chops to defrost.'

'At least you won't starve and that's the main thing,' he said lightly, closing the fridge door. He glanced at his watch and sighed. 'I'd better get a move on otherwise I'm going to be late.'

'Yes, of course. Have a nice time and say hello to Rachel for me,' she said quickly, doing her best to behave as though everything was fine.

'Will do.' He paused in the doorway and Lisa saw an expression of indecision cross his face. 'Sure you'll be all right on your own, Lisa? I'm certain Rachel wouldn't mind if you came along.'

'Thanks but as you told me yourself two's company and three is one too many.'

It was an effort to smile but not for the life of her would she let him see how much it hurt to think about him and Rachel spending the evening together. 'I intend to have something to eat then put my feet up for the rest of evening.'

'Why don't you invite James round?'

Lisa frowned when she heard how flat his voice had sounded all of a sudden. She shot him a wary look but he just smiled at her.

'I should have said this before but I don't mind if you invite him to stay over, Lisa. Don't feel awkward about it, will you?'

'I won't. Thanks, Will.' She bit her lip but she knew that she had to return the favour even though the words seemed to stick in her throat. 'The same goes for Rachel. If you want to ask her to stay the night, it's fine with me.'

'Thanks. I'll bear it in mind.'

He gave her another quick smile then left and a few minutes later Lisa heard the front door closing. She opened the fridge and took out the carton of eggs then found a pan and set it on the stove before she realised that she no longer felt hungry. Maybe she would have a bath before she made herself something to eat.

She left the kitchen and went to her room, trying not to think about what had happened. Maybe she should have told Will that James was in Leeds at the moment. He was in the middle of a very important trial and had told her the other night at dinner that he wouldn't be able to see her until Christmas Eve when she went to the cottage.

James had phoned and left a message on her mobile phone to say how much he was looking forward to seeing her again. She knew that she should try to phone him back, but she simply couldn't face the thought of him asking her if she had made up her mind yet about what she was going to do when she was still so unsure about everything. Maybe she should have explained all that to Will while she'd had the chance?

She sighed because what difference would it have made if she had told Will that? Why should he care what she did? He had his own life to think about and he couldn't keep worrying about her all the time.

It was a strangely depressing thought and she tried not to dwell on it as she slipped out of her clothes. Will's old towelling robe was still draped over the back of the chair where she had left it so she put it on and went into the bathroom. Turning on the taps, she filled the tub then sighed when she realised there were no dry towels left. Will must have used the last one when he'd had his shower.

She took the damp towel off the rail, intending to dry it on the radiator while she soaked in the bath. She shook it out then paused when she caught the tangy scent of the soap Will always used coming off the damp cotton.

All of a sudden it struck her just how much she was going to miss sharing the everyday intimacies that were all part and parcel of them living together. It would be Rachel who dried herself on a towel that smelled of him in the future, Rachel who would wear his robe, Rachel who would share everything with him and not her.

She stared at her reflection in the steamy mirror over the basin and it was impossible to ignore the pain in her eyes. She simply couldn't bear to think of losing him to Rachel, or any other woman.

The evening was turning into a disaster. It hadn't been so bad while he and Rachel had been watching the film because it had meant that he'd been spared the task of having to make conversation. But once they left the cinema, Will found it increasingly hard to keep up the pretence that he was enjoying himself.

He kept thinking about Lisa back at the flat, and wondering if she had done as he'd suggested and invited Cameron round for the night. How was he going to feel if got home and found them there together?

The thought made him break out in a cold sweat and his damp palm slipped off the gear lever as he turned into the car park of the Indian restaurant where they had decided to eat after the film.

'Sorry,' he murmured as the car bucked in protest at such ham-fisted treatment.

He pulled up in a parking space, willing himself to calm down, but the thought of Lisa and Cameron in bed together made him feel as though a red-hot knife was being twisted in his guts. *Nothing* had ever felt this painful before!

'Not to worry.' Rachel turned to look at him and he heard her sigh. 'What's wrong, Will? And before you tell me that everything is fine, I have to say it doesn't look like it from where I'm sitting. You've hardly said a word all night.'

'I'm a bit tired, that's all. Take no notice.' He adopted a deliberately bright tone. 'Well, I don't know about you, but I'm starving. I believe the tikka marsala here is absolutely superb so I might try that. How about you? What do you fancy?'

'What I would really like is for you to tell me the truth.' Rachel put her hand on his arm when he went to open the car door. 'Why did you ask me out, Will?'

He sighed because he simply couldn't find it in his heart to lie to her. 'Because I felt it was time I got on with my life.'

'Well, at least you're honest! I'll say that for you.' She laughed softly and Will grimaced as he realised how that must have sounded.

'Sorry. That didn't come out the way I meant it to.'

He turned to her and smiled, wondering why he didn't feel anything when she smiled back. Rachel was very pretty and he could understand why many men would be attracted to her, yet he didn't feel even a flicker of interest.

His mind suddenly swooped back to those moments in the hall when he and Lisa had collided, and he had to bite back a groan. Feeling her small breasts crushed against his chest had made him long to sweep her into his arms and make mad, passionate love to her. How he had managed to resist the urge he would never know. If he hadn't moved away when he had, there was no doubt in his mind what would have happened.

All of a sudden he could picture *exactly* what would have happened. He could actually *see* himself carrying Lisa into his bedroom and laying her down on his bed. She'd been wearing one of those prim little blouses she favoured and his body spasmed with desire as he imagined undoing each tiny button until she was lying there in just her underwear…

'Tell me to mind my own business if you want to, but is it Lisa?'

Will blinked and all of a sudden he was back in the present with Rachel asking him a lot of awkward questions. 'I'm not sure I understand what you mean.'

'It's simple. Are you in love with Lisa?' Rachel shrugged when he didn't reply. 'I told you that I didn't want to step on anyone's toes when you asked me out, Will. So if you only did it to make Lisa jealous then I wish you'd tell me. I'll understand, really I will.'

'No, it wasn't like that,' he said quickly, his heart aching because jealousy was the last thing Lisa would feel with regard to him. 'Lisa is involved with someone else. He's asked her to marry him, in fact.'

'And how do you feel about the idea of her marrying this other guy?' Rachel asked gently.

'I'm pleased for her, of course,' he began, then stopped because he could tell that she didn't believe him. 'I hate the idea, if you want the truth. I know I shouldn't feel this way but I can't help it.'

'Because you love her?' Rachel sighed when he shrugged. 'I'm so sorry, Will. I know how it feels to love someone and lose them.'

Will shot her a questioning look. Maybe he should be focusing on his own feelings but it was easier not to think about himself at that moment. Was he in love with Lisa? Everything pointed towards it and yet the thought of loving her and losing her to another man was too much to bear.

'Do you want to tell me about it?' he asked gently.

'No.' She smiled sadly. 'Thanks, but there really is no point, Will. Suffice it to say that I understand how you feel. I also want you to know that I'll help any way I can, even if it's only by providing you with a cover story. Sometimes the only thing you can do is to save face and try not to embarrass yourself or the other person, isn't it?'

'Yes, you're right. And there is no way that I want to embarrass Lisa when she is getting her life back together.'

He leant over and kissed Rachel lightly on the cheek. 'Thanks for being so understanding, Rachel. I really appreciate it. Now, how about that meal I promised you?'

They let the subject drop and went into the restaurant. However, despite what Rachel had said, Will knew it would be wrong to ask her out again. He couldn't bear to think that he was using her, even though she had assured him that she didn't mind.

In the event it was quite a pleasant evening so that by the time he dropped her off at her home, he was feeling a little better about what had happened. His upbeat mood didn't last, unfortunately. The closer he got to home, the more depressed he felt about what might greet him.

It was a relief when the hospital beeped to tell him that he was needed. Ray was the designated on-call surgeon that night but he hadn't responded when the switchboard operator had tried to contact him.

Will assured the woman that he didn't mind covering for Ray. He turned the car round and headed back along the bypass, feeling as though he had been given a reprieve. At least now he wouldn't know whether or not Cameron had spent the night with Lisa. It was a small comfort at least.

'Will you be taking him back to Theatre this afternoon?'

Lisa took the chart off the end of the bed and handed it to Dave Carson. It was two minutes past six in the morning and she had only just come on duty when Dave had arrived. The anaesthetist wanted to check on a child who had been admitted to the unit during the night and was scheduled for further surgery later that day.

Seven-year-old Liam Donnelly had been rushed to the hospital after police had been called to his home. Neighbours had alerted them after they had heard the boy screaming. It appeared that the boy's stepfather had beaten him for wetting his bed.

The child had suffered several fractures along with a range of other injuries including a ruptured spleen and was in a critical condition. It had been deemed too risky to transfer him to Manchester, the nearest paediatric intensive care unit, so the decision had been made to admit him to Dalverston despite the current MRSA scare.

Lisa knew that it must have been difficult to weigh up the pros and cons and couldn't help wondering who had made the final decision. She'd not had time to read the child's case notes which would have provided the answer.

'Who decided to send him to us instead of transferring him to Manchester?' she asked as Dave handed back the child's notes.

'Will. He operated on him and it was his decision to send him here.' Dave shook his head as he looked at the boy. 'It was touch and go whether the poor kid would make it, apparently. Will obviously decided that it would be too big of a risk to move him.'

'I didn't realise Will had been called in,' Lisa exclaimed, then blushed when Dave shot her a questioning look. It was obvious the anaesthetist must have heard the relief in her voice.

She busied herself with putting the boy's notes back in the holder. Discovering that Will's bed hadn't been slept in when she had got up that morning had caused her more than a little heartache. It hadn't taken her long to reach the conclusion that he must have spent the night with Rachel. Finding out that he had been right here in the hospital made her feel as though a weight had been lifted off her shoulders all of a sudden.

'Why do I get the impression that it was good news to hear that Will had been here, working his socks off? You're not developing sadistic tendencies like the rest of us, I hope, Lisa?'

'I was just worried what had happened to him when I discovered that his bed hadn't been slept in,' she said lightly, hoping that Dave would take what she said at face value.

'You mean he didn't go home after he finished here?' Dave looked momentarily puzzled before he suddenly grinned. 'Ah, I see! Wait till I see Will. The sly old dog!'

'What do you mean?' Lisa asked, frowning.

'Will left here just after two. Mike Carruthers was the on-call anaesthetist last night and he happened to mention what time they'd finished when I passed him in the foyer on my way in. Will would have had plenty of time to go home to bed but he obviously had other plans.' Dave winked at her. 'Give you two guesses where he spent the night.'

'You mean he stayed at Rachel's?' she said, her heart sinking once more.

'Rachel? Do you mean Rachel Hart?' Dave laughed when she nodded. 'Brilliant! I've been dying to find out who he's been seeing. Wait till I tell Madge. She'll be tickled pink when she hears that it's Rachel he's been dating!

'Anyway, I'll come back later to see how Liam is doing. I'm not happy about him having another general anaesthetic at the moment, so we might need to leave pinning his femur for a day or so. The poor kid has had the stuffing knocked out of him all right. Let's hope the police lock up the stepfather and throw away the key.'

Dave didn't give her a chance to say anything else as he hurried away, leaving Lisa miserably aware that she might have broken a confidence. She had no idea how Will would feel when he found out that she'd been the one to tell Dave about Rachel.

She went to the office to read through the notes Sanjay had left for her. He was always very thorough so it was a long report about what had gone on during the night. She tried her best to concentrate but her mind kept skipping about all the time, always coming back to the same problem of what she was going to do.

Will must be serious about Rachel if he'd spent the night with her because he wasn't the kind of man who would go in for one-night stands. In all the time she had known him, in fact, she couldn't remember him ever having an affair.

She frowned because that thought struck her as odd. Will was a very attractive man in the prime of his life and there must be a lot of women who would be thrilled to go out with him. Yet since Gareth had died, he hadn't even been out on a date. Why? Because he hadn't wanted to get involved with a woman when so much of his time had been taken up by her?

She sighed because it hurt to know how much he had given up for her sake. It made her see that the only way she could repay him for all that he had done was by giving him the space to get on with his life. Now that he had found Rachel and they were obviously making a commitment to one another then it was time she moved on. Maybe it would be best for everyone if she accepted James's proposal.

The telephone rang and Lisa jumped. She snatched up the receiver, wondering why she felt so relieved about not having to make a decision right at that moment. The sooner she made up her mind the better yet she couldn't quite bring herself to make the final decision to marry James.

Maybe it wouldn't hurt to put it off until after Christmas. Another week or so wouldn't make that much difference.

CHAPTER SEVEN

IT WAS mid-morning before Will realised there was something going on. He had been vaguely aware of an undercurrent in Theatre but had been far too busy to worry about it.

The infection control team had cleared all the theatres now and he was trying to catch up with some of the elective surgery which had been postponed. It had been rather like working on a conveyor belt as one patient after another had been wheeled in. Now when he looked up and caught Madge Riley and Dave Carson staring at him he sighed.

'OK, so what's going on? You two are like a couple of kids on Hallowe'en. I keep expecting you to shout ''Trick or treat?'''

'Why should you imagine there's anything going on?' Madge said loftily. She quickly collected the swabs he had used and set them aside on the trolley to be counted then went to the corner of the room where the stereo was set up. 'How about a little mood music to soothe us all?'

Will raised his eyes. 'I didn't need soothing until you two started playing up.'

'Tut-tut, Mr Saunders. It's not like you to be so snappy.' Madge poked a gloved finger at the power button and switched on the machine. 'Anyhow, this should help to calm you down.'

Will decided that the best thing to do was to ignore them and bent over the operating table again. Five-year-old Katie Tomkins was having a myringotomy, a procedure in which an incision was made in the eardrum and a small tube—called a grommet—was inserted.

Katie had a history of ear infections which had resulted in glue ear, a condition in which the middle ear cavity became blocked with sticky secretions. This had led to a loss of hearing which had been picked up when the little girl had been given a routine hearing test at school.

The grommets, which Will was in the process of inserting, would equalise the pressure on both sides of the eardrums and allow the mucus to drain down the Eustachian tube. The grommets would then fall out of their own accord in six to twelve months' time.

It was the kind of routine surgery which he had performed more times than he could count, but it would make such a huge difference to Katie's life to be able to hear clearly that it was very worthwhile.

He carefully inserted the tiny tube into the child's right ear then frowned when he realised which song was playing in the background. Glancing up, he shot a questioning look at Madge who had returned to her customary place at his side.

'You must have dug this one up from the bottom of the pile. I can't remember when I last heard this song. Enjoying a little nostalgia trip this morning, are we, Sister?'

'Oh, I just thought it was highly appropriate in the circumstances.' Madge's eyes twinkled at him over the top of her mask.

'What circumstances?' he asked blankly, wondering what she was getting at.

'Your little *liaison* last night, of course,' Dave chipped in. He hummed a few bars of the melody then chuckled. 'So, was it an enchanted evening, then, Will? And before you try to deny what you were up to, I have it on very good authority that you didn't go home last night. That naturally led me to conclude that you must have spent the night somewhere else. Am I right?'

'Oh, you're certainly right.' Will's tone was clipped because it hurt to know that Lisa had been gossiping about him. It had to be Lisa who had told Dave that he hadn't gone home—who else? Yet what would she think if she found out how wrong she had been about where he *had* stayed?

He cut off that thought, knowing it was pointless to hope that she would be pleased to learn that he had spent the night on the sofa in his office and not in Rachel's bed. He simply hadn't been able to face the thought of going back to the flat and discovering that Cameron was staying there so had taken the easy way out.

In the event he had slept well enough, but the thought that people were now adding two and two and coming up with an answer that bore no resemblance to the truth, thanks to Lisa, stuck in his throat. How could she have started such an unsavoury rumour about him?

'I slept in my office last night and before you say anything, my secretary will vouch for the fact.' He treated Dave to a frosty look. 'I nearly frightened the life out of her when she walked in this morning and found me. So, whatever fanciful notions you've got into your head, I suggest you forget them.'

'Right. Um…sorry.' Dave sounded sheepish but Will wasn't feeling kind enough to worry about the other man's feelings. In his heart he knew that Dave and Madge hadn't meant anything by their teasing but it didn't help.

He finished the operation in silence, steadfastly ignoring the lilting music issuing from the stereo. In no way could he describe his evening as having been *enchanted* although he couldn't vouch for what Lisa's evening had been like, of course. Had it been wonderful for her to have Cameron sharing her bed?

The thought made him want to throw up but he wasn't a man given to such extreme behaviour and he refused to indulge in it now. He thanked Madge and Dave in his usual courteous fashion then went through to change into fresh scrubs. He had another three operations scheduled before lunch, but all of a sudden he realised that he needed a few minutes' breathing space before he started on the next one.

'I'm taking a break,' he explained tersely as Dave followed him out. 'You may as well do the same. Tell the others that I'll expect them back here in fifteen minutes time, will you?'

'Sure,' Dave agreed readily. 'About what just happened, Will—'

'Forget it.' Will didn't give him the chance to apologise purely because he didn't want to have to deal with how it made him feel to think about Lisa gossiping about him.

Stripping off his gown, he left the theatre and made for the stairs, taking them two at a time as he ran up to the canteen, two floors above. His legs were a little stiff from yesterday's jogging session but he ignored the aching muscles. All he needed was a cup of coffee then he would be back on track.

Elbowing the canteen door open, he joined the queue at the counter and asked for a large cup of black coffee when it was his turn. The place was packed with staff having their morning breaks and the thought of having to share a table and make polite conversation was the last thing he felt like doing.

He paid for his drink then headed out of the canteen and made for the terrace instead. It was bitterly cold outside and he really wasn't dressed for such weather, but he wanted to be on his own. He needed to get his head round the idea that Lisa didn't even care enough about him not to start spreading rumours.

His vision blurred and he quickly raised the cup to his mouth and swallowed some of the fortifying liquid. He had to get a grip on himself and he had to do it sooner rather than later. He could either deal with what was happening or he could let it completely ruin his life...

Only it was already ruined because Lisa was leaving him for another man.

'So there you are. I've been looking *everywhere* for you, Will!'

He swung round when he recognised Lisa's voice, feeling his heart fill with sudden warmth when he saw the concern on her face. Had she been worried when she hadn't been able to find him? he wondered. And was it a sign that she truly cared about him, perhaps?

The thought was so mind-blowingly marvellous that it was all he could do to stop himself sweeping her into his arms and telling her how he felt.

'I owe you an apology, Will. I've done something awful and I'll understand if you're angry with me.' She took a deep breath then hurried on before he could say anything, the words tumbling over each other in her haste to get them out.

'I told Dave about you and Rachel. I didn't mean to. I swear. It just sort of…well, slipped out. I'm really, really sorry, Will. Can you ever forgive me?'

Lisa bit her lip but the grim expression on Will's face filled her with dread. It was obvious that he was angry with her and who could blame him? Rumours like the one she had unwittingly started could spread through the hospital at the speed of light. He must be furious with her for having put him and Rachel in such a difficult position.

'Will, say something!' she pleaded when he remained silent. 'Even if it's only to shout at me. I never, *ever* meant to cause you and Rachel any embarrassment. I swear!'

'It doesn't matter.' He drained his coffee-cup then strode towards the door, pausing when she failed to move out of his way.

'I can't let you go like this! I can tell you're upset and it's all my fault.' She put her hand on his arm when he went to step around her and gasped when she discovered how icy cold his skin felt. 'You're freezing! You shouldn't be out here in those clothes. You'll catch your death.'

Her gaze swept down his body then back up again but somehow it seemed to have absorbed a surprising amount of detail from that single glance. Lisa felt little bubbles of awareness fizz along her veins as she recalled how the green scrub suit had moulded itself to his body. There was quite a strong breeze blowing across the terrace and it had plastered the thin cotton fabric against his muscular chest and thighs. Quite frankly, Will might have been standing there stark naked for all the good the clothing was doing!

'I'm fine. I appreciate your concern but there is no need to worry about me, Lisa, I assure you.'

The flat note in his voice slowly got through to her and she raised worried eyes to his face. It wasn't like Will to be so unforgiving. Normally, he was the first person to want to resolve an issue, the one who played peacemaker whenever there was a dispute. It made her wonder if it was just her unthinking remark that had upset him or something else she had done. All of a sudden it seemed important that she should find out the truth.

'Will, what's wrong?'

'I'm sorry, but I have to get back,' he said, brusquely interrupting her. He stepped aside so that she was forced to release him and opened the door to go back inside.

'I really am sorry, Will,' she said softly, hating the thought that he was still angry with her. On the few occasions they had disagreed in the past they had quickly resolved their differences, but this was different. This didn't just involve him and her but Rachel as well. Was Will unable to forgive her because she had upset the woman he loved?

The thought was so painful that tears stung Lisa's eyes but she blinked them away. She was a grown woman, not a child, and if she had done something wrong then she had to admit it. There was no way that she would let him think that she was trying to play on his sympathy.

She stood up straighter when he glanced back, but it was one of the hardest things she'd ever had to do, to face the fact that he was more concerned about Rachel's feelings than he was about hers.

'I shall apologise to Rachel as well when I see her. The last thing I want is to cause trouble between you two. I wouldn't like her to think that you were the one to start everyone gossiping.'

'You don't need to worry about that,' he said tersely. 'Rachel will understand.'

'Of course.' She summoned a smile but she couldn't deny how foolish she felt. 'Obviously Rachel won't think it's your fault. She must know that you would never discuss your relationship. Just tell her that I'm sorry, though, will you?'

'Yes.'

He didn't say anything more before he hurried back inside. Lisa followed more slowly, shivering as she stepped back into the warmth. She hadn't realised just how cold she had grown through standing outside.

She went to the canteen and bought herself a cup of hot chocolate, hoping it would warm her up. Most of the staff had finished their breaks by now so she managed to find an empty table and sat down. She wrapped her hands around the steaming mug but icy shivers kept on passing through her system.

She sighed because the chill owed itself less to the outside temperature than to the frosty reception Will had afforded her. Having him treat her so coolly would take a lot of getting used to, but she had to accept that the situation had changed dramatically in the past few days. Rachel was the one he cared about now and there was little room left in his life for her. The sooner she accepted that, the easier it would be.

Her hands shook as she picked up the cup because she knew how difficult it would be to follow that advice. Accepting that Will was in love with another woman wasn't going to be an easy thing to do.

Daniel Kennedy's parents were waiting to see her when Lisa got back from her break. Daniel had shown some small signs of improvement during the night but he was still very ill and she knew how worried they must be. She took them into the relatives' room, smiling when Angela arrived a few seconds later with cups of tea for everyone.

'Thanks. Will you stay?' she asked the ward sister, knowing that it would help the parents to hear Angela's views on the progress their son was making. At a time like this, parents needed every bit of reassurance they could get. She turned to the couple as Angela drew up a chair.

'First of all I wanted to tell you that we are extremely pleased with the way Daniel has responded to the new antibiotic treatment. It's very encouraging.'

'So you do think he's responding then, Dr Bennett?' Jane Kennedy said hopefully.

'Oh, yes. I know it's difficult for you to tell how he is doing, but we are able to assess Daniel's condition far more accurately and he is definitely improving.' Lisa turned to Angela. 'You agree, don't you, Sister?'

She waited while Angela briefly outlined the small improvements which had been noted in Daniel's condition, things like a drop in his temperature and his blood pressure rising.

'And that's good, is it, Doctor? They are positive signs that he is on the mend?'

'Indeed they are.' Lisa smiled reassuringly at Brian Kennedy, the boy's father. 'Obviously, Daniel has a long way to go before he gets better, but he is heading in the right direction at last.'

'I don't understand how he got this infection,' Jane put in. 'I spoke to my sister last night and she said that he must have caught it here in the hospital, but surely that can't be right?'

'It's one possibility,' Lisa conceded. 'MRSA is a problem in a lot of hospitals, although I'm happy to say that there hasn't been an outbreak at Dalverston General for a number of years. We have a very strict infection control policy here and that has helped to prevent an outbreak.'

'Then if Daniel hasn't caught this disease in here, how has he caught it?' Brian asked, frowning.

'MRSA isn't a disease but a strain of bacterium,' she explained. 'Basically, everyone has *Staphylococcus aureus* bacteria on their skin. The bacteria can also be found everywhere in the environment but for healthy people they don't cause a problem. It's only if you cut yourself or maybe get bitten by an insect—anything that breaks the skin, in fact—that you might suffer a minor infection as a result of *Staph*.'

'But if these bacteria aren't really dangerous, why are they making Daniel so ill?' Jane asked worriedly.

'Most *Staph* infections aren't dangerous because they can be treated with simple antibiotics,' she clarified. 'However, the strain which is causing Daniel to be so ill no longer responds to those antibiotics. The bacteria have become resistant to them and consequently cause more of a problem.'

'Why has it happened, though, Dr Bennett?' Brian put in.

'I'm afraid it's all due to the way antibiotics have been over-prescribed in the past. Many bacteria have altered their structure and are now resistant to the more widely used antibiotics. Unfortunately, it means there are only a few antibiotics left which we can use to treat MRSA.'

'But Daniel is responding to the new treatment, isn't he?' Jane said quickly.

'He is. I've prescribed vancomycin for him and it seems to be working, although I must warn you that he will need to be on antibiotics for some time. We need to be sure that the bacterium won't cause him any problems in the future.'

She gave the parents a moment to digest all that then stood up. 'Now shall we go and see how Daniel is doing? I know it's a bit of a chore, having to put on a gown and a mask every time you visit him, but it's vital that we stop the infection spreading to the other children.'

'How does it spread?' Brian asked curiously, following her from the room. 'Is it a bit like a cold germ?'

'Yes, it is. It can be passed on through respiratory droplets as well as carried on your hands or in the equipment we use.' Lisa paused outside the side room to where Daniel had been moved.

'That's why Sister is so keen on people washing their hands and pays such close attention to making sure that everything is sterilised after use. The standards of hygiene here in the intensive care unit are some of the highest I've ever come across.'

'That's what I told my sister,' Jane said firmly, taking a gown from the pile outside the door. 'I told her that Daniel couldn't be in better hands and I meant it. He's lucky to have you looking after him, Dr Bennett, and very lucky it was that wonderful surgeon who operated on him. I doubt Daniel would still be with us if it weren't for him.'

Lisa smiled but it was hard not to let her feelings show as she listened to the woman praising Will. He *was* wonderful and not only in his work but in all sorts of ways. She couldn't help wishing that she had realised it sooner and acted upon it. Then he might not have needed Rachel in his life.

She bit back a sigh as she led the way into the room because that was just wishful thinking.

Will was glad when lunchtime arrived. Normally, he enjoyed his job to such an extent that he could block out everything else while he was working. However, that day he had needed to make a concerted effort to stay focused. Every time he had relaxed his guard, his mind had skipped back to what had happened on the terrace.

He knew that he had been less than gracious when Lisa had tried to apologise to him. Maybe she had been wrong to tell Dave about him seeing Rachel but surely he should have accepted her apology in the spirit it had been offered?

The thought that he had upset her by his brusqueness didn't sit easily with him. He realised that he would have to find her and clear up the misunderstanding. After all, it wasn't her fault that she had been more concerned about making amends than worried when she hadn't been able to find him.

He sighed because he had never considered himself to be an overly sensitive person before. Since when had he started getting all prickly because people didn't say or do what he wanted them to? He couldn't make Lisa feel things she didn't feel and he had to accept that and not go ruining their friendship. The last thing he wanted was to spoil that when it was all they had left.

He left Theatre and headed for the changing-room, pausing when he spotted Ray leaving Theatre Two. Ray had been late arriving that morning so Will decided that he may as well take the opportunity to have a word with him about his time-keeping. And while he was doing so he would find out what had happened the previous night, when Ray had been unavailable when the switchboard had tried to page him. Taking his turn on call was all part of the job, as Will intended to make clear.

'What happened to you this morning?' he asked without any preamble as Ray joined him. 'Everyone was waiting in Theatre for you to turn up, with the patient already prepped.'

'I overslept. Sorry,' Ray said lightly.

He hadn't sounded as though he'd meant it and Will frowned as he led the way into the changing-room. He didn't want to start making an issue of this but he was becoming increasingly concerned about the younger doctor's attitude.

'Please, make sure it doesn't happen again,' he said firmly. 'It causes no end of problems if we get behind with the lists. And while we're on the subject of you turning up, what went wrong last night? The switchboard told me that you hadn't answered your beeper.'

'Was I paged?' Ray queried, looking surprised.

Will could tell that he was lying, however, and it annoyed him to know that the man was prepared to lie rather than admit that he had chosen not to respond to the call. It was the kind of behaviour he wouldn't tolerate and he needed to make that perfectly clear.

'Yes, you were. There was an emergency admission, a young boy who had been badly beaten by his stepfather and suffered some very nasty injuries. If I hadn't been able to attend, the general surgical team would have had to deal with the case and, frankly, that isn't acceptable. I expect all the members of this team to pull their weight.'

'You're making it sound as though I *deliberately* didn't respond to the call.' Ray laughed as he opened his locker door. 'I didn't get it,

Will, and that's the honest truth. My girlfriend drove up from London last night and decided that she didn't want our evening being interrupted. She switched off my beeper and I didn't discover what she had done until this morning.'

'Then may I suggest that you have a word with her and tell her not to do it again? Whoever is the designated on-call surgeon has to be available at all times.'

'Don't I know it!' Ray sighed as he took a bottle of shampoo out of his locker. 'One of the reasons why I decided to leave my last post was because I was fed up being at everyone's beck and call all the time. Every time I went anywhere there would be a phone call, asking me to go back to work. I had no personal life.'

'It's one of the hazards of the job,' Will said unsympathetically, because Ray should have known what he was letting himself in for when he had accepted the job at Dalverston. He'd been at pains during the interviews to make it clear that they had a very demanding workload but, obviously, Ray hadn't taken what he had said to heart.

'And maybe I'm just starting to realise that it's not something I'm prepared to put up with for very much longer.' Ray slammed his locker and headed for the showers, looking far from pleased about the reprimand.

Will didn't say anything because he could tell there would be no point. Ray was obviously having second thoughts about working at Dalverston and he doubted if there was anything he could say to make him change his mind.

He sighed as he followed the younger man to the showers. It looked as though they might have another vacancy in a few weeks' time. It would put all the pressure back on him, but that might not be a bad thing. The harder he worked the less time he would have to think about Lisa's imminent departure. He could immerse himself in his work until he had come to terms with it.

He grimaced. If he worked twenty-four hour days for the next umpteen years he would never get used to being without her! Still, at some point he would have to accept the inevitable. He also needed to apologise for the churlish way he had behaved that morning. It would be a shame to spoil what little time they had left together.

Will went straight to the IC unit after he had changed but there was no sign of Lisa when he got there. Angela was in her office so he knocked on the door but she had no idea where Lisa had gone to.

He went upstairs to the canteen in case she'd gone for lunch but once again he drew a blank. He headed back down the stairs, wondering where she had got to. She was always so conscientious about telling the staff her whereabouts that he couldn't understand why she hadn't mentioned where she was going that day.

He reached the floor where the children's wards were situated and hesitated, wondering if he should tell Rachel what had happened. Although he was fairly sure that Dave and Madge wouldn't gossip there was always a chance the story might get out and it seemed only fair to warn her.

He sighed as he made his way to Children's Medical because he couldn't help feeling guilty about Rachel. Asking her out last night had been a mistake and he wouldn't do it again. He would hate to think that she might end up the subject of any unsavoury gossip because of him.

He rounded a bend in the corridor and came to an abrupt halt when he saw Lisa and Rachel deep in conversation outside the office. It was obvious they were discussing something important and his heart plummeted as he found himself wondering what they were talking about. What if Rachel told Lisa how he felt about her? What would she think if she found out that he was in love with her?

His mind spun but there was no way he could avoid the truth any longer. He *was* in love with Lisa.

Will took a deep breath but it wasn't easy to decide what to do. Should he stay and try to limit the amount of damage that might be caused by such a revelation or should he simply turn tail and run? It was hard to decide, and before he could make up his mind, Lisa glanced round and saw him.

Will felt his heart sink when he saw the shock on her face. Rachel must have told her! It was the only possible explanation for why Lisa was looking at him that way.

He swallowed a groan of dismay. Now what was he going to do?

CHAPTER EIGHT

'You two look very serious. What are you up to?'

Lisa hurriedly smoothed her features into a suitable expression as Will came to join them. Discovering that Will *hadn't* spent the night at Rachel's house had come as a shock. On the one hand she was deeply relieved because the thought of him and Rachel spending the night together was so painful, but on the other hand she knew that she shouldn't feel this way at all.

Will was a free agent and she had no right to feel hurt or betrayed if he slept with another woman! And yet if she'd had to stand up in a court of law and swear that she had felt neither of those things, she couldn't have done so. It was an effort to behave as though there was nothing wrong when he shot her a searching look.

'We were talking about you as it happens.' Rachel answered the question, mercifully sparing Lisa from having to do so.

'I don't know if I like the sound of that,' he said lightly, but Lisa could hear an undercurrent in his voice and frowned.

Why did Will sound so nervous all of a sudden? Was he afraid that she might have said something to upset Rachel? Bearing in mind their earlier frosty confrontation, it seemed likely and her heart ached because it seemed to mark the deterioration of their friendship.

'I was just telling Lisa what a lovely time we had last night.' Rachel grinned at him. 'There's no need to look so worried because I wasn't trying to get her to tell me all your darkest secrets! Anyway, she's far too discreet to do that.'

'I'm sure she is.'

Once again Lisa heard the edge in his voice only this time she understood what had caused it. She'd been far from discreet that morning when she had told Dave about him seeing Rachel. She rushed to explain what she was doing there. Will was obviously dubious about her motives and the sooner she set him straight the better it would be.

'I came to apologise to Rachel for what happened this morning. As I've just explained to her, I never intended to start any rumours about you two.'

'And for the hundredth time, Lisa, it doesn't matter!' Rachel patted her arm. 'Don't go giving yourself a hard time because there is no need—is there, Will?'

'Of course not.' Will turned to her and smiled. 'I know what Dave can be like. He's the proverbial dog with a bone when he starts digging for information.'

Lisa felt her eyes prickle with tears because it was such a relief to know that Will had forgiven her. She smiled up at him, unable to hide how happy she felt. 'Thanks. I was afraid that you would never forgive me for letting slip that you and Rachel were seeing each other,' she admitted huskily.

'Don't be daft! It would take more than that to ruin our friendship.' He looped an arm around her shoulders and gave her a quick hug then just as quickly let her go again.

'Well, I'm glad that's all sorted out.' Rachel beamed at them both. 'I'd hate to think you two had fallen out because of me.'

'There's no chance of that happening,' Will said firmly, and Lisa laughed.

'Ditto. Anyway, thanks for being so understanding, Rachel. I promise that I shall be wary when Dave comes fishing for information in the future.'

'Oh, don't worry about it,' Rachel said cheerfully. 'There's a lot worse things that can happen to you than being the subject of a bit of idle gossip. Anyway, now that we're all friends again why don't we make up a foursome one night?'

'A foursome?' Lisa repeated uncertainly.

'Yes. You and your fiancé and Will and me.' Rachel lowered her voice confidingly. 'Will told me your news, Lisa. I hope you don't mind. I'm really thrilled for you.'

'Thanks, but I'm afraid congratulations are a little premature as yet.'

Lisa managed to hold her smile but it was hard to hide her dismay at the thought of Will discussing her with the other woman. Had he been so relieved at the thought that she would soon be off his hands that he hadn't been able to stop himself sharing the good news, perhaps?

'I haven't actually agreed to marry James yet so I don't think it would be right to claim him as my fiancé,' she said firmly, trying to blot out that painful thought.

'Oh, I see. I hadn't realised that.'

Lisa saw the oddest expression cross Rachel's face. She had no idea why the other woman should look so smug all of a sudden. She was just about to ask her what was wrong when Rachel turned to Will.

'You should have explained that Lisa and her boyfriend aren't officially engaged,' Rachel chided him. 'Here was I thinking the wedding was a foregone conclusion, but obviously it's not.'

'It never occurred to me,' he said flatly.

Lisa shot him a wary look when she heard the dullness in his voice and felt her heart leap when she discovered that he was looking at her. There was something in his eyes, a sort of yearning that shocked her so much that she found it impossible to look away. It was only when Rachel spoke that she managed to break eye contact and even then she could feel tremors of awareness passing through her. Why had Will been looking at *her* with such longing when it was Rachel he loved?

'Typical man, to get the facts wrong,' Rachel observed cheerfully, seemingly oblivious to what had happened. 'However, I shall forgive you on condition that you agree to take me to the staff Christmas party on Saturday. It's going to be a very up-market affair this year—black tie for the men and as much glitz and glamour as we women can supply. It will be fun to get dressed up for a change, won't it?'

'I'm not sure if I'll be free—' Will began, but Rachel didn't let him finish.

'Oh, you can't say no! I have my heart set on going.' She suddenly turned to Lisa and gasped. 'I've just had *the* most marvellous idea! Why don't you come too and bring your boyfriend? It would be the perfect opportunity to introduce him to all your friends.'

'I'm afraid that won't be possible,' Lisa said hurriedly, glad to have the perfect excuse to avoid going to the party. Although it was kind of Rachel to invite her, she couldn't cope with the thought of seeing Will and Rachel together as a couple. 'James is in Leeds at the moment. He's in the middle of a trial and needs to stay there in case anything crops up.'

'Then you must come with us. Mustn't she, Will?' Rachel didn't give him a chance to answer as she hurried on. 'That's all settled, then. It will be fun, won't it—the three of us going together?'

'Oh, but I couldn't,' Lisa protested, her heart sinking at the thought of being forced to spend the evening with them. It would have been bad enough if she'd had James with her but infinitely worse if she had to go on her own. 'It's really kind of you, Rachel, and I appreciate it, but you and Will don't want me there. I'll only be in the way.'

'Rubbish! We won't take no for an answer so there is no point arguing.' Rachel glanced round as the office phone rang. 'I'd better get that. I'll see you both later.'

She hurried into the office and closed the door. Lisa bit her lip when she saw the grim expression on Will's face. It was obvious that he was less than pleased about Rachel inviting her to go with them to the party so she hurried to reassure him. She certainly didn't want them falling out again after what had happened already that day.

'I'll make some excuse not to go, Will. It's kind of Rachel to invite me, but I don't want to play gooseberry.'

'It isn't a problem,' he said gruffly.

'But you don't really want me there,' she insisted. 'You'll have a lot more fun if it's just the two of you.'

She fixed a smile firmly into place but it felt as though her heart was in danger of breaking.

'After all, this is your first Christmas together and you'll want it to be really special.'

'And it's also *our* last Christmas together, Lisa, so how about making it special for that reason?' Reaching out, he caught hold of her hands and Lisa shivered when she felt his fingers gripping hers. Maybe it was silly but it felt as though he was trying to tell her something that he was unable to put into words.

'I'm sorry I was so short with you this morning when you tried to apologise,' he said, his deep voice grating in a way that sent a spasm rippling through her.

'It's all right,' she said a little breathlessly, because it seemed to be incredibly difficult to get any air into her lungs all of a sudden.

'I know you wouldn't deliberately spread rumours about me, Lisa. Gossiping about your friends isn't something you'd do.'

'No, it isn't.' It was hard to think when he was staring at her so intently. She had the strangest feeling that her answer was vitally important to him.

'And that's what we are, isn't it, Lisa— friends?'

'Of course.'

She gave a tinkly laugh, wishing that she knew where this was leading. Her heart gave a sickening jolt when it struck her that maybe he was asking for her blessing. Did Will want her to tell him that she was happy because he had found love with Rachel and that she released him from his obligation to Gareth?

It made such perfect sense that she wondered how she hadn't seen it coming. Will's innate sense of duty wouldn't let him shirk his responsibilities and it was up to her to tell him that he was free to get on with his life.

'Your friendship has meant such a lot to me, Will. I doubt I would have got over Gareth's death if you hadn't been there for me, but now it's time we both moved on, isn't it?' She smiled up at him but inside her heart was weeping because this was the most painful thing she'd ever had to do.

'Now that I've met James and you've found Rachel, the situation is bound to change. I hope that we can always remain friends, though. I'd like to think that we'll be able to meet up in years to come and reminisce about the old days.'

She reached up and kissed him lightly on the cheek and it took every scrap of courage she possessed to smile at him when she felt like crying her eyes out because of what she was losing. In that moment she knew that nobody could ever replace Will in her affections, not even James. He was just too special.

'I hope that you and Rachel will be really happy together because it's what you deserve. You are a very special man, Will Saunders. The best friend anyone could ever have.'

Will could feel a burning pain twist around his heart when he heard Lisa say that. Maybe it had been foolish to hope for something more but he was only flesh and blood. He had come so close to telling her how he really felt but now he could see what a mistake that would have been. Lisa thought of him purely as her friend and he had to be content with that because there wasn't anything else.

'It means a lot to hear you say that,' he said huskily.

He gave her hands a final squeeze then let her go because it was too big a test of his self-control to continue holding them. Glancing along the corridor, he gave himself a moment to collect himself before he turned to her again, but it was an effort to behave as though everything was fine when it was a long way from being that.

'How's Liam Donnelly doing? Dave said that he wasn't happy about him having another general anaesthetic so we've rescheduled his op for Friday.'

'So-so.' Lisa grimaced. 'I'm glad you didn't transfer him to Manchester because I don't think he would have survived the journey. We're having problems stabilising him, I'm afraid.'

'He took a real hammering,' Will said darkly, thinking about the state the boy had been in when he had seen him last night. 'Has his mother been in to visit him yet?'

'No. There's been no sign of her. There hasn't even been a phone call, in fact.'

Lisa sighed and he saw her hazel eyes fill with sadness. 'How can any mother let that happen to her child, Will? It's something I shall never understand even though this isn't the first time I've come across a situation like this. I would fight tooth and nail to protect my children.'

'I'm sure you would. I'm also sure that you wouldn't get involved with a man who would present a threat to them either,' he said bluntly.

'I hope so, too, but it isn't always easy to foretell how a person will act. Maybe Liam's stepfather seemed nice enough at first and only changed after his mother married him,' she suggested.

'It's possible, I suppose.' He frowned because that idea had touched a nerve. He couldn't help worrying about how well Lisa knew James Cameron. Granted, they had been seeing each other for a couple of months now, but was that really long enough to get to know someone properly?

'I'd better get back before they send out a search party to look for me,' Lisa declared, checking her watch.

Will tried to quieten his concerns by reminding himself that she was unlikely to fall in love with a man who would treat her badly, although maybe it wouldn't hurt to make a few discreet enquiries about Cameron. It shouldn't be *that* difficult to find people who knew him.

He swallowed a sigh because he knew in his heart that he mustn't interfere. Lisa was old enough to look after herself and he had to accept that she knew what she was doing, even though it wasn't going to be easy to stop worrying about her. His life had revolved around making sure that she was safe and happy for so long that it was going to be a hard habit to break.

'I'd better get a move on, too.' He quickly checked his own watch because there was no point getting caught up on the thought of how difficult it would be to adjust to not having her around. 'I've just given Ray a dressing-down for being late so I'd better try to set a good example.'

'It must be hard work, being above reproach all the time, Mr Saunders,' she teased.

'Believe me, it is!' He rolled his eyes when she laughed, trying not to dwell on how lovely she looked. Even though she was only wearing work clothes, she still managed to look fantastic.

It made him wonder what she would look like on the night of the Christmas party, all dressed up for the occasion. All of a sudden he realised that he wanted to go to the party with her and spend what would probably be their last evening together. It seemed only fitting that it should be special, memorable.

'You will come to the Christmas party, I hope,' he said before he could think better of it. 'It might be the last chance we have to spend an evening together. You'll be moving out of the flat soon and, after that you'll be too busy planning the wedding.'

'I haven't accepted James's proposal yet,' she reminded him, and he frowned when he heard the quaver in her voice.

'But you're going to, aren't you, Lisa?' he said quickly, hoping that his urgency didn't show. Had she decided that Cameron wasn't the right man for her after all? His foolish heart raced at the thought.

'I expect so.' She gave him a brilliant smile. 'After all, James is quite a catch, isn't he? A woman would need to be mad to turn him down.'

'She would indeed.' Somehow he managed to return her smile as his hopes were dashed again. Lisa was going to marry Cameron and he had to accept that and not keep hoping it wouldn't happen.

'In that case, you definitely must come to the party,' he said, adopting a deliberately cheerful tone which was completely at odds with the way he was feeling. 'Look on it as a last fling before you settle down to being a respectable, engaged woman!'

She laughed at that. 'Implying that I'm not respectable at the moment? Thank you very much. And I thought you were supposed to be my friend! Anyway, I'll think about it. But now I have a job to do so I'll see you later.'

She gave him a last smile then hurried away. Will waited until she had rounded the corner before he started to follow her. He stopped when Rachel poked her head out of the office door.

'Before you go, Will, I think I owe you an apology.'

'What for?' he asked uncertainly.

'For putting you on the spot like that about the Christmas party.' Rachel grimaced. 'I just thought that if we all went together then you'd have a chance to get to know Lisa's boyfriend. I know how you worry about her and thought it might help. I had no idea he would be away on the night and it felt mean to take back the invitation when Lisa told me. Sorry!'

'It doesn't matter,' he assured her. 'It was kind of you to try to help.'

'I'll understand if you don't want to go, though.' Rachel looked wistful all of a sudden. 'It's been ages since I went to the Christmas party and it would have been fun to go this year.'

'Then I'll get tickets for all three of us,' he said firmly, hating to disappoint her.

'So Lisa has decided to go after all?'

'Yes.' Will frowned when he heard the satisfaction in Rachel's voice. He shot her a wary look but she simply smiled at him. 'I managed to persuade her in the end. Anyway, I'll sort out all the arrangements and get back to you. OK?'

'Fine,' Rachel agreed, going back into her office and closing the door.

Will hesitated, wondering why he had the feeling that he was missing something. He gave himself a brisk mental shake. Rachel was far too open to be planning anything.

He quickly made his way to his office to check if there had been any messages for him. His secretary had a mountain of letters that needed his signature so he did them while he had the chance. He'd just reached the bottom of the pile when there was a knock on the door and Ray appeared, carrying an envelope with his name written on it.

'I've brought you this, Will. It's my letter of resignation. I've decided that I may as well cut my losses and move on.'

'I'm sorry to hear that, Ray. Are you sure you won't reconsider?'

'No. I should have made the decision months ago.' Ray shrugged. 'I'm just not cut out for sainthood, unlike you, Will. I need some fun in my life and I'm not going to achieve that if I carry on doing this job. I've been in touch with that friend I told you about and he's going to arrange an interview for me with his firm. Hopefully, this will be the last Christmas I ever spend working nights!'

Will sighed as Ray left. Losing Ray would put them under a lot of pressure. He could only hope that Ray would fulfil his duties until he had finished working out his notice, but if the man's past performance was anything to go by he wouldn't hold his breath. Maybe he should forget about going to the Christmas party because it could turn out that he would be needed to cover for Ray again as he had last night.

He picked up the phone to ring Rachel and explain that he had changed his mind about going to the party then paused. If he cancelled their arrangements, he wouldn't be able to spend the evening with Lisa, would he?

He gently replaced the receiver in its rest. Maybe he was making a mistake but he needed this one, last memory to hold onto in the future.

'Are you going to the Christmas party, Lisa?'

Lisa looked up as Angela came into the office and plonked a pile of dressings on the desk. It was almost time for them to go home, but she was making a last-ditch attempt to catch up with some paperwork. There had been one crisis after another that afternoon so that she'd barely had time to draw breath.

Liam Donnelly had given them all a scare when he had stopped breathing. It had taken them ages to get him back and he was being closely monitored. Shock and blood loss had caused most of the damage and Lisa desperately wished the boy's mother would visit him because it might help if Liam knew she was there.

She'd only just gone back to the office when Ben Carlisle, their young houseman, had come to fetch her because Chloë Trent had had a seizure. It wasn't uncommon for a child to have fits after a serious head injury but it was still worrying and terrifying for her parents, who had been at her bedside when it had happened.

Lisa had got one of the nurses to take them into the relatives' room while she'd dealt with Chloë, administering anti-convulsant drugs to control the attack. The child would need to stay on the drugs until they were sure that she wouldn't suffer another episode.

Calming down the child's worried parents had been a major task and it had taken her some time to convince them Chloë wasn't about to die. She had explained that the fits would hopefully stop as Chloë improved, but she hadn't been able to promise that the child would never have another one. Mandy and Alan Trent had been naturally distraught and when she had left them, they had been blaming themselves for the accident. All in all it had been a hectic day and she sighed as she tossed her pen onto the blotter.

'Yes, I'm going if I'm not worn to a frazzle beforehand. What a day it's been!'

'I know. It's been mad even by our standards,' Angela declared cheerfully. 'Still, at least the party is something to look forward to, a bit of a break from the usual grind. Who are you going with, by the way?'

'Will,' she replied automatically.

'Oh, good. I'm glad he's going. He works far too hard and needs to take some time for himself.' Angela stacked the dressings into a cardboard box then looked at her. 'At least he has you around to make sure that he doesn't overdo things, Lisa. Knowing Will, he would work every hour that God sends unless someone was there to call a halt. That man is just too conscientious for his own good!'

'He is. I only hope that Rachel will keep tabs on him when I move out of the flat and stop him doing too much,' she observed worriedly.

'Sorry. I'm not with you.' Angela abandoned her dressings and stared at her. 'What do you mean, you're moving out of the flat. And who is Rachel?'

'Oops, me and my big mouth again!' Lisa clapped a hand to her mouth in dismay. However, there was no point not telling Angela the rest of the story when she had let so much slip.

'Will is going out with Rachel Hart from Children's Medical,' she explained. 'Although I'd appreciate it if you didn't tell anyone, Angela. They don't want the news spreading around at the moment.'

'My lips are sealed,' Angela promised, but she looked puzzled. 'So the reason you are moving out of the flat is because Will is seeing Rachel? Have I got it right?'

'Yes and no.' Lisa sighed because it was obvious that Angela had no idea what she meant. 'I'm not moving out because of Rachel but because I decided it was time I gave Will some breathing space.'

'Do I take it that something happened to prompt this sudden decision?' Angela queried.

'The man I've been seeing asked me to marry him,' Lisa explained. 'It seemed like the right time to make the move, basically.'

'I see. Obviously, I'm way out of touch because I had no idea that you were dating anyone, let alone that it was serious.' Angela was having difficulty hiding her surprise. 'Mind you, the same goes for Will. I just assumed that you and Will were a couple.'

'No, we're just friends. That's all we've ever been.'

It was an effort to pretend everything was fine when it felt as though her heart was breaking. It was a relief when Angela excused herself and left, although Lisa couldn't help wondering how many other people had assumed that she and Will were an item.

To an outsider their relationship must appear to be far more than it really was. They lived together so people had naturally assumed they were a couple. It made her realise what a shock it was going to be for everyone if she married James and Will married Rachel.

She took a deep breath but there was no point trying to avoid the truth. She might marry James and Will might marry Rachel. She should be happy that everything was working out so well for them both. However, it was hard to feel happy when it meant that Will would be sharing his life with another woman.

CHAPTER NINE

THE days flew past so that Will found himself wishing on more than one occasion that he could find a way to make time stand still. He was very aware that every day that passed brought him one day closer to Christmas.

Normally he looked forward to Christmas and enjoyed all the hustle and bustle, the chance it gave him to catch up with his family. However, this year all he could think about was Lisa spending Christmas with Cameron. If anything was guaranteed to make him wish that Christmas would never arrive, it had to be that!

He worked harder than ever in an effort not to think about it, staying late in his office to catch up with paperwork and putting in extra hours in Theatre while he whittled away the waiting list. It was only when Dave dryly asked him if he was aiming to get himself into the record books for the most number of operations performed in the shortest length of time that Will realised he had to call a halt. He had to stop hiding behind his work and face what was happening. Lisa was going to marry Cameron. End of story.

He picked up the tickets for the staff Christmas party on the morning of the event. He'd been lucky to get them because as soon as people had heard that the party was to be a special occasion and not just the yearly run-of-the-mill event, there had been a rush to buy tickets.

Will went back to his office and phoned Rachel to tell her that he would collect her at seven that evening. He was just about to hang up when she reminded him that it was black tie for the men.

He sighed as he put the receiver back on its rest. He didn't even possess a bow-tie let alone a dinner suit to go with it, which meant he would have to go out and buy one. For a moment he found himself wishing that he'd never agreed to go to the party before he reminded himself of all the benefits he would gain from the evening. Spending this last night with Lisa would make it all worthwhile.

Four hours later he arrived home, laden with parcels. Fortunately, he'd been so far ahead with everything that he had been able to give himself the afternoon off and had spent it in Manchester, shopping.

Amazingly, he'd managed to find a dinner suit which fitted him in the first shop he had visited and had had equal success finding a shirt and tie plus a smart pair of black shoes. It had left him with enough time to do his Christmas shopping so he had bought presents for his family—a cashmere jumper for his mother and a new golf bag for his father, gift vouchers for his sister and her husband because they would appreciate being able to choose what they wanted for their new house.

He'd added a few other bits and pieces, like a silk scarf for his secretary, luxury chocolates for the theatre staff and some toys to go in Santa's sack when presents were handed out to the children on Christmas morning. He'd decided to buy Rachel some perfume because he appreciated her kindness and he was hoping that she would like the one he had chosen. Lisa's present had been the last thing he'd bought, although he still wasn't sure whether or not he should give it to her.

He took the parcels into his bedroom and dumped them on the bed. Digging into his pocket, he pulled out a slim leather box and opened it. As soon as he had seen the necklace in the jeweller's window he'd known it would be perfect for Lisa. The delicate, gold filigree chain was set with tiny seed pearls and diamonds and would look stunning on her. The only problem was that he wasn't sure how she would feel about him giving her such an expensive present when they normally exchanged much more modest gifts. Would she be embarrassed to receive it from him?

He sighed as he closed the box lid and slid it into a drawer. If only he could give her the present *and* tell her how he felt, but he couldn't do that. He had to keep his own counsel and if giving her an expensive gift was out of the question then he had to be sensible about it. He could always buy her something else if he changed his mind, but right now he needed to start getting ready.

He took a deep breath but he couldn't deny that he was suddenly excited about the coming evening. Obviously, he had to pay as much attention to Rachel as he did to Lisa because Rachel was supposed to be his partner tonight. However, the thought of dancing with Lisa and holding her in his arms made his insides churn with anticipation. He intended to make this night one he would always remember!

Lisa was about to leave work that night when Liam Donnelly's mother turned up. It had been extremely busy in the intensive care unit for the past few days because Ben had been off sick with flu. Lisa had filled in for him a couple of evenings, staying on until Sanjay had come on duty.

It had been a relief not to have to spend too much time at home, if she was honest, although Will had also seemed to have been extremely busy. She'd seen him only briefly in passing and had not really had time to speak to him for several days. A couple of times she'd wondered if he had been avoiding her but as she couldn't think of any reason why he would want to do so, she had dismissed the idea.

When Ben had gone off sick she had toyed with the idea of telling Will that she wouldn't be able to go to the Christmas party, but something had held her back. Maybe it would be difficult to watch him and Rachel enjoying themselves together, but the thought of spending this last evening with him was too tempting to resist. Once she went to the cottage with

James everything would change. Whilst she knew that she should be happy at the thought of her new life, she couldn't deny that she felt sad about what she was losing.

When Angela came to tell her that Liam's mother wanted to see her, Lisa found it hard to hide her annoyance. Liam had been in the unit for several days now and it was the first time the woman had been in to see him. She found it difficult to comprehend how anyone could be so callous and uncaring about her own child.

'I expect you're wondering why I haven't been to see Liam, aren't you, Doctor?' Sarah Donnelly sank onto the chair and looked pleadingly at Lisa. She was a smartly dressed woman in her early thirties. However, the lines of strain on her face were clear to see. 'You must think I don't care what's happened to him, but I do!'

'It isn't my place to pass judgement,' Lisa said coolly, sitting down behind the desk.

'Maybe not, but you're only human. You're bound to have wondered why I haven't been in touch.' Sarah Donnelly ran a trembling hand over her hair. 'John wouldn't let me come here, you see. He said that I had to choose between him and Liam and that if I came to visit him then we'd be finished. I...I waited until he'd gone out then phoned for a taxi to bring me here, but I'll have to get back soon.'

'Are you saying that Liam's stepfather forbade you to visit him?' It was hard to keep the incredulity out of her voice and she saw Sarah Donnelly's face crumple.

'He's so jealous of Liam! He says that I care more about Liam than I do about him. I've tried everything I can think of to reassure him but it makes no difference what I say.'

'But surely your first duty has to be to your son?' Lisa pointed out. 'Liam is only seven and he needs you to look after him.'

'But what will I do if John leaves me? How will I manage then?' Sarah took a tissue from her bag and blew her nose. 'I've been on my own before, Dr Bennett. Liam's father walked out on us when Liam was a baby and I remember how hard it was to manage. John didn't mean to hurt Liam, I swear. He just got carried away.'

'To the extent that Liam might have died as a result of the beating he gave him?' Lisa shook her head. 'I'm sorry but no amount of financial security is worth putting a child through that for.'

She stood up, knowing that she was in danger of saying too much. It wasn't her place to sit in judgement, although she intended to tell the social worker in charge of the case everything that Sarah Donnelly had told her.

She sighed because it was Liam who would end up getting hurt if the social services department decided to take him into care. How could a seven-year-old be expected to understand that his mother didn't love him enough to put his welfare first?

'I'll take you through to see Liam now,' she said shortly. 'He's still very ill, but I'm sure it will help him if he knows you're here.'

'I can't stay long,' Sarah said, anxiously checking her watch. 'John will be home soon and I don't want him finding out that I've been here.'

'I can't force you to stay, Mrs Donnelly. But I strongly urge you to think long and hard about where your responsibilities really lie.'

Lisa didn't say anything else as she took the woman into the ward and handed her over to the staff nurse on duty. She left straight after that and caught the bus home. The meeting had left a bad taste in her mouth so that it was hard to summon any enthusiasm for the coming evening. Could she really cope with watching Will and Rachel together?

She frowned as she got off the bus and walked the rest of the way home. Why was it so difficult to accept that Will and Rachel were together? She liked Rachel and knew that Rachel would try to make Will happy so what was the problem?

Lisa's hand froze in the act of unlocking the front door. She took a deep breath but all of a sudden her heart was pounding. Was it possible that she loved Will not just as a friend but as a man?

Will was attempting to fasten his bow-tie when he heard Lisa's key in the lock. He sighed as he pulled one end of the black silk and the bow promptly unfurled itself.

He should never have let that salesman talk him out of buying a ready-made bow-tie because it would have been a lot easier than this. Maybe Lisa would help him? She certainly couldn't make a worse job of it then he was doing!

He went out to the hall and frowned when he realised that she still hadn't come in. Striding to the door, he whipped it open and looked at her in surprise. 'What are you doing, standing out there?'

'I...um...the lock seems to be jammed,' she murmured.

'Really?' Will frowned because he'd had no trouble getting in when he'd arrived home. 'Here, give me your key and I'll try it. Maybe your key's a bit worn and you need to get another one cut.' He went to take it off her then stopped when she shook her head.

'No, it's fine. Don't worry. It's probably me just being stupid.'

She went to hurry past him but it was obvious that something had upset her. Without stopping to think, Will put his hand on her arm and drew her to a halt.

'What's happened, Lisa? I can tell you're upset.'

'I'm fine,' she denied quickly, but he could tell it was a lie.

'You're not fine at all,' he said firmly. 'I want to know what's wrong, so tell me.'

'L-Liam Donnelly's mother came to visit him,' she said huskily, avoiding his eyes. 'She told me that his stepfather had forbidden her to see the boy because he's jealous of him. I suppose it just upset me a bit.'

'No wonder!' Will sighed as he reached out and hugged her.

'Don't!' she snapped, shrugging him off.

'Sorry.' He let his arm fall to his side and looked at her in dismay. He couldn't have counted the number of times he must have hugged her in the past and not once had she objected before.

'No, it's me who should apologise, Will. I'm sorry.' She gave him an apologetic smile but he could see the troubled light in her hazel eyes. 'I just didn't want you crushing your shirt when you're looking so smart this evening.'

'I'd look better if I managed to sort out this wretched tie,' he replied lightly, although he knew for a fact that it had been an excuse. Lisa didn't want him to hug her because it made her feel uncomfortable to have any man apart from Cameron showing her affection. It was an effort to hide how much that thought hurt.

'I don't suppose you're any good at bow-ties, are you?'

'I've never tried to tie one, but I'll give it a go if you want me to,' she offered immediately.

'Great! Come and read the instructions first. I'm not saying they'll help but one can only hope.'

He led the way into his bedroom and sat down on the dressing-table stool while she read through the instructions that had come with the tie. His heart filled with tenderness when he saw the tip of her tongue peeping between her lips as she struggled to make sense of them. Her soft brown hair had started to come free from its pins and he felt a little fizzing start in the pit of his stomach when he saw how the silky tendrils had curled around her face.

Did she have any idea how adorable she looked? he wondered. Could she sense how much he wanted to take her in his arms and hold her?

He sighed softly because letting her know how he felt was out of the question, especially after the way she had reacted when he had tried to hug her. However, it wasn't easy to keep a rein on his emotions when he loved her so much.

'It's as clear as mud,' she announced at last, looking up. 'Does this mean that you wrap the right side over the left first, and which is the right side exactly? If I'm facing you then my right is your left.'

'You're asking *me* a question like that?' Will groaned, hamming things up for all he was worth because he was terrified that she would guess how he was feeling. 'You're talking to the man who hasn't a single drop of sartorial elegance in his entire body! I shall leave you to decide which way it works and I promise that I won't say a word if it ends up in a mess.'

'I'll hold you to that, Will Saunders, so be warned!' She laughed and he was relieved to see that she looked far less strained all of a sudden. 'OK, then, we'll give it a go. If you're game, so am I. Now, sit up straight.'

'Yes, ma'am!'

He sat up, trying not to smile when he saw the concentration on her face as she stood in front of him. Lisa gave everything her full attention, whether it was working out the best treatment for a seriously ill child or tying a bow-tie. It was no wonder that he loved her so much.

'You'd better fasten your top button first,' she scolded. 'If I do manage to tie this, I don't want you fiddling with it afterwards and ruining all my hard work.'

'Would I do such a thing?' he replied, rolling his eyes.

He quickly fastened the neck of his shirt and grimaced as he felt the starched collar rubbing his skin. 'I hate shirts like this. They make me feel as though I'm trussed up like a Christmas turkey.'

'You have to suffer if you want to look smart,' she declared unsympathetically, sliding the length of black silk around his neck.

Will felt a spasm shoot through him as he felt her fingers brush the back of his neck. He took a deep breath but every cell in his body suddenly seemed to be on red alert. Lisa was standing so close to him now that he could smell the scent of her hair and feel the warmth of her skin. He had an overwhelming urge to put his arms around her and hold her, keep her there and never let her go, only he didn't have the right to do that. Cameron was the only man who was allowed to hold her now.

A knifing pain shot through him at the thought of the other man holding her in his arms as he longed to do. It was an effort not to show he was upset when she looked up.

'Now, from what the instructions seem to say you have to pass this end over that one then loop it through here like this…'

Once again the tip of her tongue peeped between her lips. Will, unsuccessfully, tried to swallow his groan. Why hadn't he realised how stressful this was going to be? It was the sort of test no red-blooded male could ever hope to pass.

'Are you all right?' She stopped and looked at him in concern. 'I've not pulled the tie too tight, have I?'

'No, it's fine. I've just got a bit of a tickle in my throat and I was trying not to cough,' he fudged, using the first excuse that came to mind. He cleared his throat in the hope that it would give a bit more credence to the lie and saw her frown.

'I hope you're not sickening for something. Ben has been off with flu for the past few days. Evidently, there's a lot of staff off sick with it at the moment. Do you have a temperature?'

Lisa laid her hand on his forehead and Will almost choked for real this time. It felt as though an electric current had passed through his system. He could feel his heart racing, his pulse pounding, his blood pressure soaring. And as for the rest of him... Well!

He willed himself to calm down but the throbbing in the lower part of his body refused to obey. He took a deep breath, praying for enough will-power to help him through this moment. How would Lisa feel if she realised that he was sexually aroused because she'd taken his temperature?

'You do feel rather warm.' She lowered worried hazel eyes to his. 'How do you feel, Will? Do you think you're sickening for something?'

'I'm fine,' he said hastily. 'If I feel hot it's because I've been struggling with this pesky tie and got myself into a real lather about it.'

'Well, don't worry about it. I'm sure we can sort it out between us.' She treated him to a reassuring smile then turned her attention to the task at hand.

Will let out a heartfelt sigh of relief at having escaped detection. He shifted slightly, praying that the loosely cut trousers would hide the evidence of his arousal. He *couldn't* and *wouldn't* embarrass Lisa by letting her see how much he wanted her.

'I'm going to start this again right from the beginning,' she declared, unfastening the tie. 'It can't be *that* difficult to tie this wretched thing. Now, hold still while I give it another go.'

She bent towards him again and sighed. 'I just can't seem to get close enough to see what I'm doing properly.'

'Is this better?'

Will parted his legs so that she could stand between them then immediately realised his mistake when his body instantly responded again to the intimacy of their position. He tried breathing deeply but there was no way that an extra supply of oxygen was going to have any effect when Lisa was standing so close that they might have been making love...

He shot to his feet, uncaring about what she thought as he brushed past her. He wanted her so much that it was pure torture not to be able to do anything about it.

'Will, what's wrong?' she asked uncertainly, and his heart almost came to a halt when he heard the alarm in her voice. The thought of her shock and dismay if he told her the truth was more than he could bear. Lisa thought of him as her friend so how on earth could he explain that he ached to be her lover?

'A touch of cramp, that's all,' he lied, turning away so that she couldn't see his face. He hated having to lie to her but what choice did he have? He couldn't ruin their friendship by telling her the truth.

He summoned a smile as he glanced round, feeling his insides knot with longing as he looked at her, standing there. He wanted to

sweep her into his arms and make mad, passionate love to her, then make love to her all
over again only slowly and tenderly this time.
She was his whole world but he loved her too
much to hurt her by telling her that. All he
could do was be glad that she had found happiness at last, even if it wasn't with him.

'Anyway, it's late and you need to get ready.
I'll give it another shot myself.'

'If you're sure...?' She shrugged when he
nodded. 'OK. But I'll try again after I'm
dressed if you still haven't managed to do it.'

She picked up her bag from his bed and suddenly spotted the parcels which he'd left there.
'Looks as though you've done your Christmas
shopping.'

'I thought I'd get it over and done with while
I had the chance.'

He went to the dressing-table and picked up
his cuff-links, watching her in the mirror as she
studied the heap of brightly wrapped gifts. A
tender smile curved his mouth because Lisa
took an almost childish delight in giving and
receiving presents at Christmas.

'No peeking!' he warned. 'It won't do you
any good because your present isn't there. I've
hidden it.'

'Meanie!' she accused. 'Fancy making me wait until Christmas Day to see what you've bought me.'

'I won't see you on Christmas Day, remember? You can have your present on Christmas Eve.'

It was an effort to hold his smile as the full enormity of what was happening hit him afresh. Lisa wouldn't be with him on Christmas Day. She would be with Cameron after having spent the night with him. How could he bear to think about Cameron making love to her when he wanted to be the one to do so?

All of a sudden Will knew that he had to tell her how he felt and stop her leaving him. He couldn't go on if Lisa wasn't with him. Life would have no meaning without her there beside him. He swung round then jumped when the phone beside his bed suddenly rang.

Lisa reached for the receiver and listened for a moment. 'He's right here. Hold on.' She offered him the phone. 'It's Rachel for you. I'll go and get ready while you talk to her.'

Will took the receiver but it was several moments before he managed to lift it to his ear. Even then his hand was trembling so much that it was difficult to hold it steady, harder still to respond to what Rachel was telling him.

He hung up, wondering what to do. Rachel had phoned to tell him that she couldn't go to the party because her niece was ill and she wanted to stay with her. It meant that he and Lisa would have to go on their own, but might it not be better in the circumstances to cancel their plans?

He had come so close to telling Lisa the truth about how he felt just now and he knew what an awful mistake that would have been. It would have ruined their friendship because Lisa would have been too embarrassed by such a revelation to let it continue.

If they went to the party, could he trust himself not to make the same mistake again? Could he be certain that he would be able to keep control of his emotions? And yet if they didn't go, how could he cope in the coming years when he desperately needed this one last, wonderful memory to see him through all the lonely times ahead?

CHAPTER TEN

Lisa stood in front of the mirror and studied herself critically. She'd spent ages looking for a dress for the party on her last day off and she still wasn't sure if the one she had chosen was right for the occasion. It was certainly far more sophisticated than anything she'd ever worn before.

Her eyes skimmed assessingly over the rich, burgundy-red velvet. The dress was simply cut with long sleeves and a high neckline. The narrow-fitting skirt ended just below her calves so that from the front the dress looked extremely demure. It was only when she turned and glimpsed the back in the mirror that she realised how daring it really was.

The entire back of the dress consisted of a network of interlaced satin straps which extended from her nape to her waist. She could see the pearly sheen of her bare skin through the straps and frowned. Was it *too* sophisticated perhaps and not really her? What would Will think? Would he like it?

She turned to face the mirror again and picked up her hairbrush, trying to calm the rush of adrenaline that had surged through her. The whole time she'd been getting ready she had refused to think about what had happened earlier, but it was impossible to blot it out now.

Was she in love with Will? Or did she simply love him as a friend?

She had no idea what the answer was and it scared her to think that she couldn't make up her mind about something so important. If she was in love with Will then how could she marry James? Yet how could she *not* marry James when it might mean that Will would continue to feel responsible for her?

She sighed because whatever decision she reached would affect somebody. She hated to think that she might hurt James if she decided not to marry him, and she certainly wouldn't be able to live with herself if Will ended up getting hurt. She had to decide what would be the right thing to do for everyone concerned.

She finished brushing her hair and picked up the tiny velvet evening bag lying on the end of her bed. It was barely big enough to hold her comb and a lipstick, but it was such a perfect match for the dress that she hadn't been able to resist it. She'd even bought new shoes for the occasion—strappy evening sandals with wickedly high heels which she probably wouldn't wear again. However, she'd wanted to look her best tonight, even though Will would be far more interested in what Rachel was wearing.

It was a rather deflating thought but she tried not to think about it as she went to find him. He was looking out of the sitting-room window and didn't appear to have noticed her coming into the room. Lisa paused in the doorway, thinking how handsome he looked in the formal evening clothes. The tailored, black jacket emphasised the width of his shoulders while the starched, white evening shirt was the perfect foil for his dark hair. He'd even managed to fasten his bow-tie, although she couldn't help smiling when she noticed that it was just a little bit crooked at one side.

A wave of tenderness washed over her because if Will had looked too perfect, it wouldn't have felt right. Will wasn't the kind of man who spent time worrying about his appearance. He was always far too concerned about other people to think about himself. Rachel was so very lucky that he had fallen in love with her.

He must have sensed she was standing there because he suddenly turned. Lisa drove that painful thought from her head when she saw his eyes widen. She gave him a tentative smile but she couldn't deny that her nerves were humming with tension as she waited to hear his verdict. Would Will think that she looked beautiful that night, perhaps?

'You look wonderful, Lisa. That dress is just perfect.' He crossed the room and she felt her pulse race when she saw the admiration on his face.

'You think it's all right, then?' she asked, loving the way his eyes crinkled at the corners when he smiled at her.

'Rather more than ''all right''! You look fantastic.'

'You don't look too bad yourself,' she replied, struggling to keep control of her pulse before it beat itself to death. Maybe it was silly to set so much store by Will's opinion, but she couldn't seem to help it.

'Thank you kindly. But what about the tie? Is it OK?' He started to twitch one end of the bow-tie but Lisa quickly swatted his hand away.

'Leave it alone! It looks fine and you'll only end up making a mess of it if you start fiddling with it again.'

'So long as you're sure I don't look a complete idiot,' he began, but she shook her head.

'You look wonderful, Will. Honestly. You scrub up a lot better than I thought you would!'

'That's a backhander if ever I heard one,' he declared, laughing at her.

'If you will go fishing for compliments, you should expect to get knocked back,' she retorted, although she couldn't deny that her heart was racing like crazy. Maybe it was her imagination but there seemed to be a definite tension in the air all of a sudden. Will seemed as aware of her as she was of him and it was hard not to let it affect her.

She took a steadying breath as she turned towards the door, deeming it safer not to dwell on the reason why it was happening. 'Anyway, enough of these compliments. We'd better get a move on or Rachel will be wondering where we've got to.'

'Rachel isn't coming, I'm afraid.'

Lisa swung round. 'She's not coming? But why on earth not?' Her heart suddenly sank as a thought occurred to her and she looked at him in dismay. 'It hasn't anything to do with me, has it?'

'No, of course not!' he denied immediately. However, Lisa wasn't convinced.

'Are you sure? Look, Will, I would far rather you told me the truth. If Rachel has had second thoughts about me going with you then just say so. I don't want to spoil the evening for you both.'

'It has nothing whatsoever to do with you,' he said firmly. 'Rachel isn't going because her niece is ill. Rachel is the girl's guardian and, naturally, she wants to stay at home and look after her.'

'Oh, I see. What a shame that she's going to miss the party, although I expect I'd feel the same in her place.'

Lisa felt a wave of disappointment wash over her because there was no way that she could expect Will to take her to the party now. He'd only offered to do so because Rachel had asked her to go. 'It seems we've got all dressed up for nothing, doesn't it?'

'We're still going, Lisa.' He frowned when she looked at him in surprise. 'That's if you still want to go?'

'I do, but are you sure that you want to go now that Rachel won't be there?' she said slowly. 'It won't be the same without her.'

'Of course not, but it would be a shame for all of us to miss the party.' He smiled but Lisa had seen the sadness in his eyes and bit back a sigh. It was obvious that Will was disappointed that Rachel wasn't able to go with him but, typically, he didn't want to spoil the evening for her.

'After all, this night was supposed to be special for a number of reasons, Lisa. It's probably the last chance we'll have to spend much time together so let's go and enjoy ourselves.'

'Why not? It sounds like a good idea to me.' Lisa summoned a smile because she didn't want him to know how much it had hurt to be reminded that they would be going their separate ways soon.

'Then what are we waiting for?' He stepped aside and bowed low. 'Cinderella *shall* go to the ball!'

Lisa laughed but her heart was heavy as they left the flat and drove to the hospital. There were just two days left before she was due to go to the cottage. Maybe she should be looking forward to it and making plans for the future, but all she seemed able to think about was how much she was going to miss Will. Leaving him for any reason wasn't going to be easy.

The party was being held in the hospital's gymnasium and the staff social committee had worked miracles, transforming it for the occasion. All the equipment that was normally used in there by the physiotherapy team had been cleared away and the whole room had been decorated with boughs of greenery from which were hung red and gold streamers.

Tables had been brought down from the canteen and draped with sheets, and there were red and green candles in wine bottles on every one. Lisa was amazed by the transformation and said so as Will handed over their tickets at the door and escorted her inside.

'It's fantastic! I never imagined the place could look this good.'

'It's certainly different to how it looked yesterday when I came to see how young Andrew Brown was getting on with his physio.' He sniffed appreciatively. 'It even smells different. There's none of that liniment aroma which is usually the first thing you notice when you come in here.'

'That's because of all the greenery,' she said, glancing up as they passed under an archway of spruce placed just inside the main doors.

Will looked up and grinned when he saw a large bunch of mistletoe strategically placed above the entrance. 'Somebody has obviously caught the Christmas spirit.'

Lisa laughed. She was about to move on when he caught hold of her hands and turned her to face him. 'Happy Christmas, Lisa,' he said softly.

Lisa felt her breath catch as his mouth found hers. The kiss lasted no longer than a couple of seconds but she was trembling when he let her go. She pressed her hand to her mouth as Will moved on to let the next people in the queue take their turn under the mistletoe but she was deeply shaken by what had happened.

She felt her heart start to race as she stared after him. If Will loved Rachel then why had he kissed *her* with such passion?

He should never have done that!

Will could feel himself breaking out into a cold sweat as he crossed the room. Lisa was still standing by the door and he longed to look back at her yet dreaded what he would see. Had she realised that kiss had been far more than the token she would have expected from him?

He ground his teeth in frustration because there was nothing he could do about it now. He should have kept a tighter rein on himself but the moment he'd felt her soft mouth under his it had been impossible to control his emotions. It was a relief when Dave Carson came hurrying over because it meant that he didn't have to deal with what he had done right then. However, there was no way that he could forget about it when it might have all sorts of repercussions.

'We've got ourselves a table in the corner,' Dave informed him, pointing across the room.

Will summoned a smile when he saw Madge waving to him. 'At least we'll have somewhere to sit down. The place is really packed tonight.'

'Every ticket has been sold, apparently. That's why Jilly and I decided to get here early and grab some seats. Right, I was just on my way to the bar so what are you having?' Dave frowned as he looked towards the crowd of people who were filing into the room. 'Where's Rachel got to? I can't see her anywhere.'

'She couldn't come,' Will explained tersely because Lisa had joined them.

His heart sank as he watched her greeting Dave then make her way across the room to where the rest of their party was sitting. It was obvious that she had deliberately avoided looking at him and he could only draw his own conclusion from it. It was an effort to respond when Dave asked him why Rachel hadn't come.

'Her niece is ill and she wanted to stay at home with her,' he explained, struggling to control his panic. Had Lisa worked out why he had kissed her like that? Had she realised that he was in love with her? The thought made him feel light-headed with fear because he had no idea how she might react to the revelation.

'That's a shame,' Dave said sympathetically. 'Still, at least you've got the whole of Christmas to make up for her not being here tonight. Lucky you to have managed to get both Christmas Day *and* Boxing Day off!'

'There has to be some perks for being the head of the department,' Will observed dryly, doing his best to behave as though nothing was wrong. 'There's certainly a lot of disadvantages that go with the job.'

'Like having to keep an eye on our newest recruits, for instance,' Dave said acerbically.

Will frowned. 'Do you mean Ray? What's he done now?'

'It's what he hasn't done which is more to the point. He never turned up again this afternoon. We were all ready in Theatre, waiting for him, and he just didn't show up.' Dave sounded grim. 'I could throttle him, to be honest. There's nothing worse than having to tell a kid's parents their child's operation isn't going ahead after they've psyched themselves up for it. It's really stressful for them.'

'It is and I can understand why you're annoyed,' Will agreed, sighing. 'I'll have a word with Ray, although I'm afraid it will be a waste of time. He's handed in his resignation,' he explained when Dave looked at him quizzically. 'He's after a job with a pharmaceutical company so I don't imagine he's overly concerned about blotting his copybook here.'

'Good riddance is all I can say. We can do without staff like him, although it does mean that you're going to be pushed until we can find a replacement.' Dave clapped him on the shoulder. 'Right, enough of all that. We're here to enjoy ourselves not talk shop all night. What are you drinking?'

Will gave his order then went to join the others. Madge greeted him warmly, patting the chair next to her in an invitation to sit down.

'Thanks.'

Will smiled around the table but he was very aware that Lisa was still ignoring him. Had she worked it out yet and realised what had been behind that kiss? he wondered. The thought that he might have ruined their friendship made him feel quite ill so that it was an effort to respond to Madge's questions about Rachel's whereabouts.

'She wanted to stay at home with her niece. Apparently the girl isn't feeling well and Rachel didn't like to leave her on her own,' he explained once again.

'It's a shame she couldn't come,' Madge said sympathetically. 'Rachel is such a love. There's not many women who would put their lives on hold to bring up their sister's child, like she's done. Still, it looks as though things might change for the better for her in the not too distant future.'

Madge winked at him then turned to speak to Dave's wife, Jilly. Will sighed because he couldn't help feeling guilty about letting everyone think that he and Rachel were an item.

His gaze moved to Lisa and he felt a sharp pain pierce his heart. If only he could tell Lisa the truth, it wouldn't matter what anyone else thought!

Lisa knew that Will was watching her. She could feel his eyes on her in a way that shouldn't have been possible. Nobody could actually *feel* a look yet she could feel him watching her.

She knew to the split second when he looked away as Dave arrived with their drinks, and breathed a sigh of relief. She had to put what had happened into context and not start making too much of it.

So Will had kissed her under the mistletoe. Big deal! It was what thousands of people did each Christmas and it didn't mean anything. And yet it felt like a big deal to her. Even now she could feel the tingling imprint his lips had left on hers and had to bite back a moan of dismay because, try as she may, she couldn't simply dismiss that kiss.

'Lisa?'

She jumped when Will leant across the table and set a glass in front of her. 'Thanks.' She lifted the glass to her mouth, hoping the alcohol would steady her nerves. She had to calm down and not let him see how confused she felt but it wasn't easy to pretend that nothing had happened.

'I hope it's OK,' Will said, picking up his own glass of lemonade and looking at her over the rim. 'I wasn't sure what you wanted but I know you prefer white wine to red so I told Dave to get you that.'

'It's fine,' she assured him.

She took another sip of the wine then put the glass on the table because her hand was shaking so hard that she was in danger of spilling it. That comment had touched a nerve because it had brought it home to her just how well Will knew her.

He didn't need to consult her to know that she preferred white wine to red. It was the same for her because she knew his tastes just as well. They could have appeared on one of those television game shows as the perfect couple and answered questions about each other, but their relationship had always been that of friends, not lovers. But if that was true then why had he kissed her that way? It didn't make sense.

It was an effort to concentrate as the conversation flowed around the table when that thought kept playing in the background all the time. Lisa did her best to join in but it was a relief when the music started. Dave whisked Jilly to her feet, ignoring her protests that she didn't think her feet could stand him trampling all over them.

'It's all part and parcel of being married, my love.' He leered at her. 'You have to put up with a bit of pain occasionally to stop you overdosing on the pleasure of being my wife!'

Everyone laughed when Jilly groaned as Dave swept her onto the dance floor. Madge had got up to dance with her husband, Harold, and Angela was trying to persuade her fiancé to get up as well. Lisa knew that Will would ask her to dance any minute and quickly stood up.

'I'm just popping to the loo,' she explained to nobody in particular, and beat a hasty retreat.

She made her way through the gyrating couples and took refuge in the ladies' lavatories. There was nobody else there so she went to the mirror and renewed her lipstick, even though it didn't need freshening up. She was simply putting off the moment when she would have to go back to the party and dance with Will. How would it feel to have him holding her in his arms?

A shudder ran through her because she could imagine only too easily how it would be. His skin would be warm to the touch and the heat from it would warm her, too. His hand would be pressed against the small of her back as he guided her round the floor, his fingers lightly brushing her bare skin through the interlaced straps.

Lisa's breathing quickened as the scene unfolded in her mind's eye. He would smell of soap and shampoo—nothing fancy or expensive—just that wonderfully clean scent that was purely Will's own. Halfway round the dance floor he would look down at her and smile, and his eyes would fill with tenderness because he cared about her so much.

Will was her friend, her rock, her port in a storm, and everything he had ever done had been aimed at making her happy. He had given her so much over the years and he had done it willingly and with love, and it was *that* which made it so easy to get confused. Will loved her as his best friend, as Gareth's fiancé, but he didn't love her as a man loved a woman. He couldn't.

Lisa stared at herself in the mirror as the pictures inside her head slowly faded. Will could never love her the way he loved Rachel. It made her see how foolish it would be to imagine that kiss had meant anything.

Where *was* Lisa?

Will checked his watch once more. It had been a good twenty minutes since Lisa had disappeared. Dave and Jilly were still dancing but Madge and her husband had abandoned their attempts, claiming that they couldn't keep up with the beat.

Angela and her fiancé, Graham, were deep in conversation with a couple at the next table which left him feeling rather conspicuous, sitting there on his own. However, that wasn't the reason why he was so edgy. He couldn't shake off the feeling that Lisa's lengthy absence had something to do with that kiss he'd given her. For the umpteenth time Will wished that he had never given in to the urge.

She suddenly appeared and his heart jolted nervously as he watched her crossing the room. The music suddenly came to an end and the DJ announced that the next dance would be a Scottish reel. Madge gave a whoop of delight as she grabbed his hand and pulled him to his feet.

'This is my kind of music! Come along, now. Let's form a circle.'

Before Will knew what was happening he found himself on the dance floor. Dave and Jilly joined them then Angela and her fiancé gave in to Madge's imperious summons to get up. People were forming circles all round the room, laughing as they tried to persuade others to join them.

Will saw Lisa shake her head when Morgan Grey tried to get her to join his group. Morgan was with his wife, Katrina, and several of the staff from the surgical team, but Lisa resisted their pleas to make up their numbers. She carried on past, heading for their table, and she might have made it if Madge hadn't spotted her.

'Over here, Lisa! Hurry up, the music's going to start at any moment.'

Will saw an expression of indecision cross Lisa's face. He realised that he was actually holding his breath as he waited for her to make up her mind. The thought that he might have ruined her evening by his lack of self-control was hard to swallow. He'd wanted tonight to be special for both of them, a time they could both look back on with pleasure, not regret.

Holding out his hand, he looked Lisa straight in the eyes, knowing that he had never done anything as difficult before in his entire life. Making himself look at her purely as a friend wasn't easy when he loved her so much, but it was the only way he could think of to make things right between them again.

'Come on now. No excuses,' he exhorted. 'If I have to suffer then you can, too!'

'Thanks a lot!' She gave a soft little laugh but Will could hear the strain it held. His heart ached because the last thing he'd wanted had been to upset her.

'That's what friends are for, isn't it?' It was an effort to keep the ache out of his voice when his heart seemed to be breaking, but it was Lisa who mattered most, her feelings that were his main concern. 'To share things with?'

'Is that a fact? Then remind me to be more choosy about who I pick for a friend in future, Will Saunders,' she retorted. She rolled her eyes when he fixed a pleading expression to his face. 'Oh, all right, then. But I'm doing this purely out of friendship, you understand?'

'Oh, I do. And I appreciate it.'

Somehow Will managed to smile as she dropped her bag on the table and came to join them. Hearing her state that friendship was all she felt for him had made his heart ache, but there was no way that he would ruin things again by letting her see how he felt.

He gave her hand a quick squeeze as she took her place beside him in the circle. 'Friends it is!'

The music started before she could reply and Will was glad. There was only so much he could take but he would learn to deal with the situation in time. So long as Lisa was happy then he could be happy, too, although it wasn't going to happen overnight. He would just have to content himself with the thought that things usually worked out in the end, even though there didn't seem to be even a glimmer of light at the end of this particularly long and dark tunnel. Maybe in a hundred years' time he would start to feel better.

He led her forward at Madge's prompting, taking her hands and whirling her round. The others were clapping in time to the music, laughing and shouting encouragement as they watched him twirling Lisa around until they were both breathless and it was someone else's turn.

They moved to the side while Dave spun Jilly round with much enthusiasm and very little grace. Will laughed and clapped and did everything possible to make it appear as though he was having a wonderful time, but he knew it was all an act.

He glanced at Lisa, standing beside him, and knew that he would remember how she looked at that moment for the rest of his life. She looked so young and lovely, so happy compared to how she had looked once upon a time.

He had achieved what he had set out to do and he had to draw comfort from that so that he could cope when she left him. Maybe she wouldn't move out of the flat for a while, but Christmas Eve would mark the end of their relationship. Once she slept with Cameron it would be the start of a commitment which he hoped and prayed would last all her life. She wouldn't need him any more after that.

Tears misted his eyes and the whirling dancers became a blur. He was going to miss her so much.

CHAPTER ELEVEN

IT HAD been a wonderful evening.

As everyone gathered on the dance floor to sing 'Auld Lang Syne' as the party drew to a close, Lisa knew that she was glad she had come. It had been fun spending time with people she liked, but the best thing of all had been spending this time with Will. He had gone out of his way to make the night special for her, dancing every dance with her until she'd had to beg him to let her sit down. She would remember this night all her life and look back on it with pleasure.

'I am absolutely *shattered*. How about you?'

She glanced round as Will came to join her. 'Completely exhausted, if you want the truth. My poor feet are *throbbing* from dancing in these high heels.'

'It could have been worse,' he told her with a grin. 'Dave might have asked you to dance and pity help your poor feet then!'

Lisa laughed sympathetically as she watched Jilly limping onto the dance floor. 'It doesn't bear thinking about! Poor Jilly's feet must be black and blue. It must be love if she's prepared to put up with Dave trampling all over them is all I can say.'

'Must be,' he agreed.

Lisa shot him a frowning look when she heard the dullness in his voice. He'd turned to speak to Angela and had no idea that she was watching him. Lisa felt her heart ache when she saw how sad he looked as Angela moved away. Will had put up a good show of enjoying himself tonight but he must have missed not having Rachel there with him.

She summoned a smile when he turned, hoping that he couldn't tell how much it hurt to know that she could never match Rachel in his affections. Rachel was the woman he loved while she was just his friend so Will was bound to feel differently about her. However, it wasn't easy to accept that she was second best.

'I've offered Angela and her fiancé a lift home—I hope you don't mind, Lisa. They've tried phoning for a taxi but they're all booked up.'

'Of course I don't mind,' she assured him. 'Angela lives in those new houses by the park, doesn't she? I remember her mentioning something about them moving in a couple of months ago.'

'That's right. We have to go that way so it's no problem to drop them off. It's a nice spot to live. You've got the park on your doorstep and the river is only a short walk away. Perfect for kids.'

Lisa nodded because she didn't trust herself to speak. Was Will thinking about starting a family, perhaps? If he and Rachel got married it would be the next, logical step, and yet the thought of him and Rachel having children together almost broke her heart. It was a relief when the DJ put 'Auld Lang Syne' on the deck.

Lisa linked arms with Will on her left and Harold on her right as everyone began to sing. She felt her eyes prickle with tears as she realised how apt the words were. Next Christmas she and Will would be merely old friends. They would be leading separate lives by then and she doubted if they would see very much of each other outside working hours.

The circle started to move and she felt Will grip her hand as everyone surged forward. A lump came to her throat because even now he was looking after her. Will was such a special person that it was no wonder she couldn't imagine living without him.

A great cheer erupted when the music came to an end. People were laughing and kissing each other. Harold gave her a noisy kiss on the cheek then Dave swept her into an exuberant bear hug and swung her round. Lisa was laughing when Dave set her back on the ground but she felt the laughter die in her throat when she found herself facing Will.

'Happy Christmas, Lisa—again.'

His lips were cool when they touched her cheek. Lisa felt her heart ache because it simply proved how right she'd been to decide that all Will felt for her was friendship. He couldn't possibly have behaved so indifferently towards her if he'd felt more than that.

'Happy Christmas,' she parroted, turning away before he could see the despair on her face.

It was a relief when the party broke up a few minutes later and everyone began to leave. Lisa walked on ahead with Angela, doing her best to pretend that everything was fine. Will was talking to Graham and just the sound of his voice in the background seemed to exacerbate her sadness. Two more days and that would be it. Once she went to the cottage with James then everything would change. Maybe she and Will could remain friends but it wouldn't be the same. He would no longer be at the centre of her life, neither would she be at the centre of his.

The thought plagued her all the way home. Fortunately the others made up for her silence as they discussed what had gone on at the party. They dropped off Angela and Graham outside their house then carried on home. Will drew up outside the flats and Lisa steeled herself not to show how upset she felt when he turned to her.

'I'll leave you here, if you don't mind, Lisa. You have got your key?'

'No, I never thought to bring it.' She frowned as he hunted through his pockets and handed her his keyring. 'But where are you going at this time of the night?'

'I thought I'd call round to see Rachel. I know it's late but I'm sure she'd enjoy hearing all about the party.'

'Oh, I see. Of course. Sorry, I didn't mean to be nosy.'

She quickly got out of the car, praying that he couldn't tell how devastated she felt. Will was bound to want to see Rachel. He must be longing to spend some time with the woman he loved yet the thought was like salt being rubbed into a raw wound.

'I won't be back tonight so make sure you lock the door,' he warned.

'Of course. Don't worry about me.' Somehow she managed to smile as she turned to close the car door.

Will leant across the passenger seat and Lisa felt her heart ache when she saw the concern in his eyes. When Will looked at her like that she could almost pretend that everything was back to normal, but it never would be now. She was no longer the most important person in Will's life. It was Rachel who could claim that honour. Even though she knew it was unfair, she couldn't help feeling hurt.

'I can't help worrying about you, Lisa,' he said softly, his eyes searching her face. 'It's not easy to break old habits.'

'I'll be fine, Will. Really.'

She smiled again, wondering how it was possible to say one thing and feel something entirely different. She wasn't fine at all. The thought of Will spending the night at Rachel's house, sleeping with Rachel in her bed, made her feel so sick that she could have wept.

It was only pride that stopped her making a fool of herself, pride and the fact that she would never forgive herself if she spoiled things for him. Will deserved every bit of happiness he could find and if Rachel was the one person who could make him happy then she wouldn't do anything to ruin things for him.

'Give Rachel my love and tell her that she missed a great evening. I'll see you whenever.'

She closed the car door and hurried inside. She ran upstairs to the flat and went straight to the sitting-room window and watched as Will drove away.

Tears welled from her eyes and this time she didn't try to stop them because there was nobody to see if she cried and nobody to care. She was on her own now and Will wasn't there.

Will drove straight back to the hospital and went to his office. He let himself in and switched on the lamp on the desk. Telling Lisa that he was going to Rachel's had been a lie and although he didn't feel good about it, he'd had no choice. He simply hadn't been able to stand the thought of going back to the flat and pretending that everything was wonderful when it was a long way from being that.

Lisa had been hurt by the way he had kissed her so coolly after they'd sung 'Auld Lang Syne', but what else could he have done? If he had kissed her the way he had longed to do she would have been shocked. It had been safer to feign indifference rather than show any real emotion.

He cursed roundly, giving vent to his frustration in a rare outburst which would have surprised the people who knew him. He'd never had any problem controlling his temper in the past but he was having difficulty doing so now. He wanted to shout and smash things in the hope that it would ease this agony he felt. He loved Lisa and it wasn't fair that he could never tell her that!

He sighed as he went to the window and opened the blind. When had anyone said that life should be fair? He could rail against fate all he liked but it wouldn't change things. Lisa was going to marry another man and at some point he would have to accept that. Yet as he stood there, looking out over the sleeping town, it felt as though he was staring into a black pit of despair.

He had no idea how he was going to get through the next two days, let alone the weeks until Lisa moved out of the flat. How could he bear to see her each day and know that it was Cameron's arms which had been around her on Christmas Eve, Cameron who had helped her rediscover the joys of being a woman?

He was only flesh and blood and the thought of another man making love to her, when he ached to be the one, was too much to bear. After Christmas he would have to find somewhere else to stay until she moved out of the flat. There were a number of small hotels in Dalverston and it shouldn't be difficult to find temporary accommodation. So long as Lisa never found out how he really felt about her, he could put up with any inconvenience.

Will closed the blind then went and lay down on the sofa. He would spend the next two nights in his office and keep out of the way until Lisa had left for the cottage. After that, he would make other arrangements and try to get his life back together, but filling the gap she left wouldn't be easy. No woman could ever replace Lisa in his affections.

The next two days were a nightmare. Lisa did her best but it wasn't easy to deal with the situation. Will had been staying at Rachel's since the party and he'd only been home to collect some clothes.

She'd been out shopping at the time and he had left her a note, telling her what he'd done. She had seen him only briefly in work when he'd visited the ward. He had been polite and friendly on each occasion but distant, and she hated having him cut her out of his life this way.

She busied herself with her work in the hope that it would take her mind off what was happening, but it wasn't easy to handle the shift in their relationship. It didn't help that she was growing increasingly nervous about spending Christmas with James.

He had phoned to give her directions to the cottage and apologised for not being able to drive her there himself. The trial was dragging on and the judge had decreed that they would need to work on Christmas Eve. It would be too late by the time James left Leeds to collect her and drive them both to the cottage, so he had decided to go straight there.

Lisa assured him that she would find her own way there by train, but she couldn't deny how worried she felt after she hung up. She still wasn't sure that marrying James was the right thing to do. She liked him and they got on well together, but was that really enough?

She tried to recall how she had felt about Gareth but, surprisingly, she could barely remember the heady excitement of falling in love for the first time. What she had felt for Gareth now seemed rather shallow and insubstantial.

He had been great fun and she had enjoyed being with him. He had been kind and caring as well, and had helped her get over her mother's death. It had been a very difficult period in her life and having Gareth there had helped her through it. But had she *really* loved him or had she simply needed the comfort of believing that she was in love?

The idea plagued her so it was a relief to go into work and not have to think about her own problems. Daniel Kennedy was making excellent progress and, although he was still confined to a side room, his infection was under control. Lisa was quietly confident that he would pull through.

Chloë Trent hadn't had any more fits and they were able to raise her level of consciousness. They had deliberately kept her sedated and it was a very tense time as they reduced the amount of drugs she was receiving. When she opened her eyes and asked for her mummy, everyone breathed a sigh of relief, and Mandy and Alan Trent were ecstatic.

The child who was still giving them the most cause for concern was Liam Donnelly. They had continued having problems stabilising him and Lisa knew that they urgently needed to do something about it. Physically, he should have been recovering by this stage but he lapsed in and out of consciousness. It was as though the boy had lost the will to live.

She had a word with Sanjay and they decided that they needed to persuade the boy's mother to visit him again. Sarah hadn't been back to the unit and the social worker in charge of the case had been unable to contact her.

Lisa decided to phone the woman herself and try to make Sarah see how important it was that she visit Liam. She put through a call but all she got was an answering-machine and she was forced to leave a message, asking Sarah to get in touch. The thought that poor little Liam might not pull through lay heavily on her heart but there was little else she could do.

The morning of Christmas Eve arrived at last and Lisa awoke to find that it was snowing. She'd managed to get the afternoon off and was planning on going straight to the station as soon as she left work.

She showered then packed an overnight bag, trying to remember everything she would need. James had told her he was expecting some friends for drinks on Boxing Day so she hunted through her wardrobe for something suitable to wear.

Her hand hovered over the burgundy velvet dress she had worn to the staff party before it moved on. She took a black crêpe dress off the rail instead and packed it in the case, feeling a lump come to her throat. She couldn't bear to wear the red dress ever again because it would remind her of Will.

She locked the case and left it in the hall so she wouldn't forget it when she set off for work. She put on a warm, apricot lambswool sweater and grey flannel trousers then added boots and her winter coat and set off. The path leading to the street had been swept by the care-taker but once she got out on the pavement she had difficulty keeping her footing. The snow was quite thick in places and several of the roads were blocked.

When the bus finally arrived it was packed with commuters. People had obviously decided to give themselves extra time to get to work because of the snowy conditions and every seat was taken. Lisa had to strap-hang all the way to the hospital, with the overnight bag banging against her shins every time anyone wanted to get on or off.

She was glad when it was her turn to alight, although she couldn't help sighing as she walked up the drive and thought about the journey planned for that afternoon. Heaven only knew how long it would take her to get to the cottage if the weather was as bad as this in Derbyshire. She had to change trains and James had warned her the service could be a little erratic at times.

'What a day!' Angela had followed her inside and Lisa saw her shiver appreciatively as they stepped into the warmth of the hospital's foyer.

'Oh, does that feel good! Our central heating isn't working and it's absolutely freezing at home. I've left Graham frantically phoning around all the plumbers in the town to find one who will come out and fix it.'

'Typical that it should happen today of all days, isn't it?' Lisa said sympathetically. She pressed the button for the lift then put her case on the floor because her arm was aching from carrying it.

'Where are you off to, then?' Angela asked, glancing at the case.

'Derbyshire. I'm spending Christmas with a friend,' she explained.

'Not friend as in *boyfriend*, by any chance?' Angela asked her, grinning.

'I suppose you could put it that way,' she agreed uncomfortably. She knew it was silly but she couldn't help feeling embarrassed at the thought of everyone knowing that she would be spending Christmas with James, and all that it implied.

'Then I hope you have a wonderful time, Lisa. You deserve it because you work so hard.'

Angela grimaced. 'Mind you I could say that about most of the staff here. Everyone seems to put in one hundred and ten per cent effort. I hope your boyfriend realises what he's letting himself in for when you get married. If he's hoping to have a wife who will be waiting at home with his pipe and slippers then he's in for a shock!'

Lisa laughed but the comment had touched a nerve. It wasn't the first time that she'd wondered how James would react to her working such long hours. It was all part of the job and she accepted that, but would James be happy about it or would he expect her to give up her job and spend more time with him?

The idea worried her because it made her see that she hadn't given enough thought to the problems they might encounter if she agreed to marry him. It would be unfair to James to spend so much time at work but it would be equally unfair to expect her to give up a job she loved. Maybe she needed to talk through all the problems with him before she made a final commitment, but going to the cottage *was* a final commitment. How could she refuse to marry him if she spent Christmas with him?

By the time they reached the intensive care unit Lisa's head was throbbing from trying to decide what to do. She took her case into the staffroom then went into the unit. Angela was busy taking the night staff's report so Lisa went to check on the children, stopping off at Daniel Kennedy's room first.

She slid a gown over her clothes and went in, smiling when she discovered that Daniel was awake. The boy should have been moved to a ward by now but they'd had to keep him in the intensive care unit to avoid the risk of spreading the infection. Lisa knew that he was growing increasingly bored with spending so much time on his own and made a point of popping in to see him whenever she could.

'And how are you this morning, young man?' she asked, going over to his bed.

'OK, I suppose.' He sighed as she checked his notes. 'When can I go to the ward with the other children, Dr Bennett?'

'I'm not sure yet. It all depends on how quickly we clear up these nasty bugs.' She smiled sympathetically. 'Are you feeling fed up because you're stuck in here all on your own?'

'Uh-huh. I've nobody to talk to when Mum and Dad have to go home to look after my little sister.' He suddenly brightened. 'Mr Saunders came to see me last night and he read me a story. That was fun. Will he come back again tonight, do you think?'

'I'm not sure,' Lisa said, trying to hide her surprise. What on earth had Will been doing here during the night? Unless Daniel had become confused about the time, of course.

'What time did Mr Saunders come to see you, Daniel?' she asked casually, not wanting the child to think there was anything unusual about Will's visit.

'I don't know.' Daniel screwed up his face as he considered the question. 'I heard the big clock on the church chiming three times after he left, though.'

'Did you indeed! It must have been very late, then.'

She smiled as she replaced the boy's notes in the holder but it was hard to hide her surprise. Daniel couldn't have been confused about the time because she'd been in the unit all the previous afternoon and there had been no sign of Will then.

What had he been up to, coming into work and reading the boy a story at three o'clock in the morning?

It was a puzzle and one which she found herself thinking about frequently for the rest of the morning. She was due to leave work at two so she decided not to take her lunch-break. Sanjay had agreed to cover for her but it would still leave them very short-staffed and she felt guilty about it. She decided that she would try to get through as much work as possible and just have a sandwich on the train.

By two o'clock Lisa had worked her way through a mound of paperwork and was ready to leave. She got up then paused as a thought struck her. Picking up the phone, she dialled Sarah Donnelly's number and left another message on the answering-machine. Maybe it would have no more effect than the last one had done but she couldn't bear to think of poor Liam lying in hospital with nobody to visit him over Christmas.

She went into the ward and wished everyone a happy Christmas then collected her coat and bag from the staffroom. It was still snowing when she reached the foyer and she found herself wondering if it really was a good idea to set off on a journey in such conditions. Maybe she should phone James and tell him that the weather was too bad for her to make the trip.

She sighed because she knew that she was looking for an excuse not to go. And yet if she didn't go, what would she do? Sit at home thinking about Will spending Christmas with Rachel? Surely it was time that she got on with her life as Will was doing?

Maybe she wasn't head over heels in love with James but they could have a good marriage if she worked at it. Love wasn't the be-all and end-all of a successful relationship. Look how wonderful her friendship with Will had been. If she could find a fraction of the happiness with James that she had found with Will then their marriage would work out perfectly fine.

She picked up her case and opened the door and if there were tears in her eyes, she refused to wonder why. She wasn't leaving Will, she was going to meet James. She should be happy about it, not sad.

Will found that he was constantly watching the clock as the morning wore on. With it being Christmas Eve there was no elective surgery scheduled that day and time was hanging rather heavily. He did his ward rounds, putting up a good show of being full of Christmas spirit as he chatted to the children and their parents.

Andrew Brown—the boy with the displaced epiphysis—was very excited about the coming visit of Santa Claus planned for the following morning. Will teased him about it.

'I thought you told me that you didn't believe in Father Christmas so what's happened? Have you changed your mind?'

'Course not!' Andrew declared, his ears turning pink. 'But you have to pretend for the sake of the little ones, don't you? I mean, *they* still believe in him and it wouldn't be fair to spoil their fun.'

'Of course not,' Will replied gravely, exchanging an amused look with Andrew's mother. 'So, what are you hoping that Santa will bring you this year?'

'A snowboard,' Andrew said promptly. 'My best friend goes to the new snowdrome and he says it's wicked!'

'Good job we got that leg sorted out, then, isn't it?' Will declared. 'You'll be able to have snowboarding lessons once everything is properly healed up.'

'It won't cause any damage to Andrew's leg if he goes snowboarding, will it, Mr Saunders?' Mrs Brown put in quickly. 'I'd hate to think that he might injure himself again.'

'There's no need to worry about that,' Will assured her. 'The metal pins will keep the epiphysis in place and I doubt if even Andrew will be able to dislodge them this time.'

He clapped the boy on the shoulder and smiled at him. 'You leave Santa a letter tonight and tell him that you can have a snowboard with my blessing!'

He moved on as Andrew and his mother laughed. The ward was packed with visitors that day as parents arrived to see their children and make arrangements to bring in their presents the following day. The staff had done a wonderful job of decorating the ward with balloons and streamers. There was even a huge Christmas tree set up by the door and Will paused to admire it.

He sighed as he studied the glittering baubles and tinsel that adorned it. Normally he and Lisa bought a tree for the flat, but this year they hadn't bothered. She hadn't mentioned getting one and he hadn't seen any point, although undoubtedly Cameron would have arranged to have a tree and all the trimmings at the cottage. Cameron would want everything to be perfect, a celebration of their coming union.

The thought was so mind-numbingly painful that he had to take a deep breath. The thought of Lisa and Cameron spending the holiday planning for their future made him want to throw up. It was an effort to respond when one of the nurses came over to wish him a happy Christmas because Will knew that he was within a hair's breadth of losing control.

He quickly left the ward and made his way to his office, struggling to hide his impatience when Dave hailed him. He sincerely hoped he wasn't going to be presented with a major problem because he didn't feel up to dealing with it. All he could think about was Lisa and her coming trip to Derbyshire.

'Is something wrong?' he asked as Dave hurried over to him.

'Jilly's just phoned. She's stuck in snow the other side of Cartmel. She's tried phoning the breakdown service but they've been inundated with calls and don't know what time they'll be able to get out to her,' Dave explained worriedly. 'I want to go and fetch her but Roger Hopkins said to have a word with you first to make sure it was OK. Tim Jackson will cover for me but it could be half an hour before he gets here and I'd like to leave straight away.'

'It's fine by me.' Will assured him. 'Even if we have an emergency admission it would take some time before we got the patient to Theatre and Tim should have arrived by then.' He frowned. 'I didn't realise the snow was that bad.'

'Didn't you have any trouble getting here?' Dave sounded puzzled. 'It took me ages just to get the car off our drive and the roads were a nightmare. It took me twice as long as it normally does.'

'I stayed the night in my office so I didn't need to drive here this morning,' Will said shortly.

'I didn't know you'd been called out,' Dave exclaimed.

'I wasn't.'

'Then what on earth were you doing, sleeping in your office?' Dave sighed. 'Tell me to mind my own business if you want to, Will, but what exactly is going on? You've not been yourself for days now. Is it Rachel?'

'No, it has nothing whatsoever to do with Rachel.'

Suddenly Will didn't have the heart to lie. His feelings for Lisa were eating him up and he needed to tell somebody how he felt or he would go mad. 'Rachel was just a smokescreen. It's Lisa I'm crazy about.'

Dave whistled. 'Well, you had me fooled all right. Although thinking about how you and Lisa looked the other night at the party, I don't know why I should be surprised. It was obvious there was something between you two. Even Jilly noticed it.'

'Lisa and I are just friends,' he denied tersely. 'At least that's the way she thinks about me.'

'And you're sure about that, are you?' Dave shrugged when he nodded. 'Well, I suppose you should know, Will. But Lisa didn't give the impression that she was totally indifferent to you the other night.'

'Then why is she going to spend Christmas with this guy? If Lisa felt anything for me, it's the last thing she'd do!' he exploded.

'Maybe she's doing it for the same reason that you let everyone think that Rachel was the woman you were interested in.'

Dave clapped him on the shoulder and grinned. 'Take it from me, Will, it's never easy to tell what is going on in a woman's mind. They don't think like we do, although I've a pretty good idea what Jilly will be thinking if I don't go and fetch her soon. I might just find myself wearing the Christmas pudding rather than eating it!'

Will laughed as Dave hurried away but it was hard to contain the excitement that was pouring through his veins all of a sudden. Was it possible that Dave was right?

His mind spun as he tried to deal with the idea, but it was simply too much to take in. He realised that he needed to see Lisa and find out the truth once and for all. He would never forgive himself if he lost her because he was too much of a coward to tell her the truth. He would tell her that he loved her and see what she said then.

Will went straight to the intensive care unit but there was no sign of Lisa when he got there. Angela was on the phone and Jackie Meredith was talking to Sanjay and Daniel Kennedy's parents. The rest of the staff must have gone for their breaks because there was nobody else around.

Will waited impatiently but he was getting a bad feeling all of a sudden. What was Sanjay doing here at this time of the day when he normally worked nights? Was he covering for Lisa? By the time Angela came out of the office he had worked himself into a real state and it was impossible to disguise the urgency in his voice.

'Where's Lisa? I need to speak to her.'

'I'm afraid she's already left,' Angela told him, frowning. 'Is something wrong, Will?'

'What time did she leave?' he demanded, ignoring the question.

'Just after two. She told me that she was catching the two-thirty to Bakewell,' Angela explained in bewilderment.

'You mean she's travelling by train and not by car?' he clarified.

'Apparently. Look, Will, if something has happened I wish you'd tell me…. Will? Will!'

Will didn't stop as he turned and raced along the corridor. It was fifteen minutes past two already but there was still a chance that he could catch Lisa if the train was late.

He took the stairs two at a time, ignoring the startled looks from the people he passed. There was no time to spare. He had to stop Lisa getting on that train. He had to tell her that he loved her before it was too late!

He reached the foyer, thanking heaven that he had his car keys in his pocket so didn't have to waste time going to his office to fetch them. His coat was upstairs but that didn't matter. He could put up with the cold and any discomfort if it meant he had a chance to stop Lisa making the biggest mistake of her life. Cameron couldn't love her as much as he did! He had to make her understand that.

He was actually opening the door when he heard his pager beeping and automatically stopped. He dug it out of his pocket and checked the display, feeling his heart sink when he saw that it was A and E trying to reach him.

He couldn't ignore it and yet if he responded he wouldn't be able to stop Lisa getting on the train.

What should he do? Should he put Lisa and this last chance of happiness first? But if he did that, could he live with himself if a child died because he had failed to do his job? Whatever he decided, someone was going to lose out.

CHAPTER TWELVE

THE train had been delayed because of snow on the tracks. Lisa waited in the station café, hoping that it wouldn't be too long before it arrived. The more time that elapsed the more nervous she was becoming.

Was she doing the right thing? Should she marry James when she didn't love him? But if she didn't marry him, what was she going to do? How would she cope when Will married Rachel?

Tears stung her eyes and she picked up the cup of tea she'd bought from the buffet and forced herself to drink a little of the tepid liquid. She had to calm down and think things through calmly and rationally. That was what Will always made her do and it had worked in the past, but, then, nothing had seemed difficult with Will there to help her. How could she bear to live the rest of her life without him?

'Lisa! What a surprise to see you here.'

She looked up when she recognised Rachel's voice, feeling her heart sink because the last thing she needed at the moment was to have to make polite conversation. 'Hello, Rachel. How are you?'

'Fine, although I'll feel a lot better once the train arrives.' Rachel sighed as she sat down. 'I was supposed to be going to Manchester to do some shopping and the train's been delayed because of the snow. I knew I shouldn't have left everything until the last minute!'

'It's typical, isn't it?' Lisa smiled sympathetically. 'You should have got Will to take you there by car the other day. It would have been easier.'

'Nice idea but I've not seen him for ages, I'm afraid,' Rachel remarked, pulling off her woollen mittens.

'But I thought he'd been staying at your house since the staff party?'

Lisa could feel her heart starting to race all of a sudden. She saw Rachel grimace and frowned. What was going on? Why had Will told her he was staying with Rachel when it hadn't been true?

'Oops, I think I may have just put my foot in it,' Rachel admitted ruefully. 'I don't know what Will has told you, Lisa, but he hasn't been staying with me.'

'But I don't understand. Why would he lie to me?' she exclaimed.

'Maybe you should ask him that,' Rachel said carefully. She shrugged when Lisa looked at her. 'I'm sorry, Lisa, but it wouldn't be right for me to break a confidence. Will must have had his reasons for telling you he was staying with me but that is something you need to discuss with him. It's about time you two sorted this out.'

'Sorted what out? Look, Rachel, I'm not asking you to betray a confidence. I just don't understand what is going on. You say that you haven't seen Will in days and yet I thought you two were serious about each other?'

'Will and I have been out for one date,' Rachel told her gently. 'There's no question of us being serious about each other. Will knows that as well as I do.'

'Then why did he lead me to believe that you two were an item?' She shook her head because she couldn't seem to understand what Rachel was telling her. 'None of this makes sense.'

'Doesn't it? It does if you try hard enough to work it out, Lisa. Will is the most honest and open guy I've ever met so why would he lie to you about me? Why would he want you to think that we had something going for us? It's really obvious if you think about it.'

Rachel looked up as a voice came over the loudspeaker and announced that the Manchester train would be leaving from platform two in five minutes' time. 'That's my train. I'd better go. I'm meeting my niece and she'll be wondering what's happened to me.'

'She's feeling better, then?' she queried, her head reeling from trying to work out what Rachel had meant. 'Will told me that she wasn't well the night of the party.'

'Beth's fine, thank you.' Rachel sighed as she got up. 'I may as well come clean and confess that there was nothing wrong with her the other night. I just wanted to give you and Will the opportunity to talk to one another. Obviously, you didn't do that but it still isn't too late. Think about it. Have a great Christmas, Lisa.'

'You, too,' Lisa responded automatically. She picked up her cup then put it down again as she thought about what Rachel had said to her. It all seemed to come back to the same question of why Will would lie to her about his relationship. Why had he led her to believe that he was in love with Rachel when it patently wasn't true?

Because he had thought it better to lie rather than admit that he was in love with her?

Her breath caught because all of a sudden everything made sense. Will would lie if he thought it was for her own good. He wouldn't be happy about it but he would do it if it meant that she wouldn't get hurt. He had been acting very strangely ever since she'd told him about James's proposal, in fact, and the more she thought about it, the clearer it all became.

Will had lied rather than tell her how he really felt about her. He had only ever wanted her to be happy and if he believed that she would be happy marrying James then he would make sure that nothing stood in her way.

Lisa smiled as a feeling of intense joy flooded through her. She couldn't be happy without Will because she loved him, and she loved him not just as a friend but as a man. She'd sensed it was so a week ago but had deliberately closed her mind to the idea.

It had been too difficult to deal with it when she'd believed that Will had been in love with Rachel. Now there was no reason to shy away from the truth: she loved Will with all her heart and nothing was going to stop her telling him that. Whether he would admit how he felt was something she would have to face when the time came, but she was no longer prepared to lie to him or to herself.

The announcer's voice came over the loud-speaker again to say that the Bakewell train would be arriving shortly. Lisa stood up. There was one thing she needed to do first before she did anything else.

The snow had caused a pile-up on the bypass and three children had been injured on their way to a matinée performance of the yearly pantomime at the local repertory theatre. Will took the most seriously injured, a little girl with a very nasty head injury, into Theatre and set to work.

Surprisingly, Ray had been on time that day and he was in Theatre Two, pinning and plating a badly broken arm. It was a bad injury and Will had been in two minds about letting Ray do it. However, he had decided in the end that, as he couldn't be in two places at once, he had to trust him.

Morgan Grey was operating on the driver of one of the vehicles involved in the collision.

Will knew it would be touch and go whether the young woman survived. The child he was operating on was apparently her daughter and he could only pray that the little girl wouldn't be left without a mother at Christmas. It all added to his feeling of desolation. Lisa would have caught the train by now and he was too late to stop her.

He worked steadily, removing the splinters of bone that had been pushed inwards by the blow to the child's skull. Although the little girl had been sitting in the rear of the car she hadn't been wearing a seat belt. She had been catapulted forward by the force of the collision and had hit her head on the dashboard. There was extensive bleeding from the blood vessels in the meninges—the membranes covering the brain—so he dealt with that then covered the wound.

The child would need antibiotics to prevent the risk of infection and close monitoring until she recovered consciousness so he sent her to the IC unit. Sanjay was there to sort everything out even if Lisa wasn't. Lisa must be almost at the cottage by now.

It was an effort to hide how devastated that thought made him feel as he thanked the staff and left Theatre. Ray had finished before him and was on his way out of the changing room.

'Everything OK?' Will asked politely, holding the door open for the younger man.

'Fine. It was a bit like putting together a jigsaw puzzle but I got there in the end.' Ray suddenly sighed. 'It made me realise why I went in for surgery, to be honest. You derive a great deal of satisfaction from doing a job like that.'

'It isn't too late to change your mind, Ray. I still have your letter of resignation on my desk and I can hold onto it for a while longer.' He clapped Ray on the shoulder. 'Why don't you think about it over Christmas and then let me know what you want to do?'

'I'll do that,' Ray said slowly. 'Thanks, Will. I haven't exactly made a sparkling impression since I arrived here and I appreciate you giving me another chance.

'Don't mention it.'

He let the door swing to as Ray hurried away but that last comment had touched a chord. If only he could have another chance to tell Lisa how he felt, he most certainly wouldn't waste it!

It was pointless wishing for the impossible so he tried to put it out of his mind as he showered and changed. It was gone five by the time he finally left. The car park was ankle deep in snow and it took him ages to start his car because it had been standing in the cold for the past two days.

He got it going at last and drove home. He turned off the engine and took a deep breath because he wasn't looking forward to going into the empty flat. The thought of spending the next two days there on his own, thinking about Lisa and Cameron at the cottage together, was almost more than he could stand. How could he bear to think about her and another man?

His heart felt like lead as he got out of the car and went inside. He unlocked the front door and stepped into the hall then froze. He could hear music playing and see that there were lights on in the sitting room. What the hell was going on?

Warily, he made his way along the hall and peered into the sitting room, stopping dead at the sight that met him. For a moment he wondered if he was dreaming as his eyes skimmed over the paper chains and streamers, the tinsel and balloons which adorned the room. His gaze finally alighted on the Christmas tree standing in front of the window and he swallowed. Where had all this come from?

'Will! I didn't hear you coming in. What perfect timing. I was just about to start decorating the tree and now you can help me.'

Will spun round and seriously thought he was going to pass out when he saw Lisa standing in the hall, smiling at him. What on earth was she doing here when she was supposed to be at the cottage with Cameron?

'What are you doing here?' he demanded hoarsely. 'Why aren't you at the cottage?'

'Because I wanted to spend Christmas here with you.'

She smiled at him and his heart began to race when he saw the expression in her eyes. Lisa was looking at him in a way that she had never looked at him before and he was almost afraid to believe what his brain was telling him. It was an effort to concentrate when she continued.

'Christmas is all about spending time with the people you love, and I love you, Will. I really do.'

Lisa felt a wave of tenderness wash over her as she saw the shock on Will's face. That announcement was bound to have come as a surprise to him but once he had time to think about what she'd said, he would be fine. She felt better than she'd felt in ages, in all honesty. She was suddenly able to think clearly and it was such a relief after the past two weeks of confusion.

'You love me?'

'Mmm, that's right. I know it's difficult to understand why I should after the way you lied to me about Rachel, but I'll forgive you. I'm sure you must have had your reasons,' she said gently.

'Who said I lied?' he asked tersely, running a trembling hand through his hair.

'Me.'

She took a slow step towards him, hiding her smile when he backed away. 'You lied rather than tell me how you feel, didn't you? You decided it would be easier if you let me think you were in love with Rachel and that way I'd marry James and live happily ever after.'

She shook her head as she took another step and this time he didn't back up. 'Sorry, but that's not how it works, I'm afraid. I can't live happily unless you're there with me, Will.'

'I... You... Oh, hell!'

Reaching out, he yanked her into his arms and enveloped her in a bear hug. Lisa closed her eyes, feeling her heart fill with joy. Will loved her. He really did. Now all he had to do was tell her that then they could start getting on with their lives.

'I love you so much,' he grated. 'I was so scared when you told me about Cameron.'

His voice broke and she held him tighter, feeling her eyes fill with tears as she realised what he must have been going through in the past two weeks. 'I'm so sorry, my darling. I never meant to hurt you like that. I just didn't realise how I felt, you see.'

She reached up and framed his face between her hands. 'I love you, Will Saunders, and it's you I want to spend the rest of my life with if you'll have me.'

He didn't say anything as he bent and kissed her but there was a world of promise in the way his mouth took hers so gently and so tenderly, so lovingly. He drew back and looked deep into her eyes and Lisa felt her emotions spill over when she saw the depth of his love for her.

'I shall love and cherish you until the day I die, Lisa. You mean everything to me. I think I fell in love with you right from the beginning but I would never admit to myself how I felt because it wouldn't have been right.'

'You mean because of Gareth?' She sighed when he nodded. She pressed a kiss to the corner of his mouth then smiled at him. 'I loved Gareth very much, Will, but what I felt for him bears no resemblance to what I feel for you.'

'What do you mean?' he said uncertainly.

'That I met Gareth at a time in my life when I desperately needed to love someone and be loved in return,' she explained gently. 'Losing my mother like that was very hard for me to deal with and Gareth helped me through it. I transferred all my feelings to him and that's why I was so devastated when he died and why I fell apart the way I did. Now I know that my feelings for him were nowhere near as deep as the ones I have for you.'

She reached up and kissed him on the mouth. She felt him shudder and smiled. 'Now, do you want to continue this conversation or shall we find another way to convince each other how we feel?'

He laughed softly. 'What did you have in mind, exactly?'

'Oh, I'm pretty sure you can guess what I'm thinking, Will. You always could read my mind.'

She laughed up at him then felt the laughter dying on her lips when she saw the way he was looking at her with such hunger, such need. Her heart was racing when he lifted her into his arms and carried her from the room. He took her into his bedroom and laid her down on the bed, and his eyes were full of so much tenderness and love that tears ran down her face.

'I love you, Lisa,' he whispered as he bent to brush his lips over hers. 'You are my whole world. The only thing I want from life is to make you happy.'

'And I'll be happy so long as I have you, Will.' She kissed him back, loving him with her eyes, wanting him to know how much he meant to her. 'You've been the best friend anyone could have had, but I'm greedy. I want more. I want you to be my lover as well as my friend.'

'Then, my lady, your wish shall be granted.'

He kissed her again only this time with so much passion that her heart melted. Wrapping her arms around his neck, she gave herself up to the sheer joy and magic of being loved by him.

He drew back and smiled when she murmured a protest. 'I'm not going anywhere. I just
want to get out of this coat.'

'Oh!' Lisa gasped, then laughed as she realised that he was still wearing his outdoor
clothes.

He unzipped his coat and tossed it onto the
chair then shed his jacket and tie. He sat down
on the side of the bed and pulled her upright.
'Your turn now.'

Grasping the hem of her apricot sweater, he
tugged it over her head and tossed it onto the
chair. Lisa felt her heart race almost out of control when she saw the desire in his eyes as he
looked at her sitting there in just a lacy bra.

Bending, he pressed his mouth to her breast
and she cried out when she felt his tongue rasp-
ing against her nipple. She closed her eyes,
struggling to contain the sudden flare of longing
that flowed through her as he turned his attention to her other breast and lavished it with the
same attention, but it was impossible to deal
with the way it made her feel to have Will loving her this way.

She twined her arms around his neck and
drew his head down to her, arching her back in
ecstasy as he kissed her breasts again then

reached behind her to unfasten the hook of her bra. Slowly, with the utmost delicacy, he drew the straps down her arms until the wisp of lace fell away and she was sitting before him naked from the waist up.

'You are so beautiful, Lisa,' he whispered, and she felt her heart spill over with love when she heard the awe in his voice.

'You're beautiful, too, Will,' she replied, reaching out to undo the buttons on his shirt. She undid one then two then found her hands had started to tremble so much that she couldn't deal with the third.

Will pressed a kiss to her mouth then unceremoniously dragged the shirt over his head and tossed it aside. 'Is this better?' he asked roughly, taking hold of her hands and placing them, palms down, against his warm, hair-roughened chest.

'Much,' Lisa whispered, her breath catching. She slid her hands experimentally over his chest then stopped and bit her lip. Being given this licence to touch him suddenly scared her because it made her see how close she had come to losing him. If she'd got on that train today, she wouldn't be here now. The thought was almost too much to bear.

'What's wrong, sweetheart? Tell me.'

His hand was so gentle as he tilted her face, his voice so full of love that tears welled from her eyes again. 'I was just thinking how close I came to losing you. If I'd got on the train...' She couldn't go on as emotion overwhelmed her.

Will drew her into his arms and cradled her against him and she could hear the ache in his voice.

'Don't even think about it! I was on my way to the station to beg you not to go when I had a call from A and E. I don't know how I made myself turn round and respond to it.'

'You were coming to find me?' she asked incredulously.

'Yes. I wanted to tell you the truth about how I felt, you see.' He sighed as he wiped away her tears. 'I had no idea if it would achieve anything but I couldn't bear to let you go without telling you that I loved you.'

'Oh, Will! We've been such idiots, haven't we? Both of us were trying not to hurt the other and yet that's what we almost ended up doing.'

'But it was "almost". We came to our senses in the end.'

'Yes, and thank heaven that we did. It would have been the biggest mistake of my life if I'd gone to the cottage.' She kissed him tenderly then smiled into his eyes. 'I phoned James and explained everything to him. He was very nice about it, too.'

'Mmm, if that's an attempt to convince me that Cameron deserves my sympathy, I'm not sure it's going to work. He's put me through hell in the last couple of weeks with that proposal of his!'

'Now, Will, it's not like you to be unkind.' She kissed him again and sighed. 'One of the things I love most about you is the concern you always show to other people.'

'What other things do you love?' he said, grinning at her in a way that made her heart race.

'Well, you're good-tempered and very easy to get on with. The fact that you just happen to be extremely handsome also goes in your favour.'

'So you think I'm handsome, do you? Good. What else?'

She rolled her eyes but there was something rather delicious about playing this game with him when she knew how it was going to end.

'You're good company and never boring. You know how to cook and—'

'Mmm, I think that's more than enough. We'll stop right there.' He pressed her back against the pillows and his eyes were filled with love as he looked down at her.

'You've convinced me that you are a woman of taste, Lisa. It would be a shame to waste any more time discussing my virtues when I have a much better idea how to utilise it.'

Lisa closed her eyes as he bent towards her. She gave a little sigh of contentment when she felt his lips find hers. Will was right because it would be a shame to waste the night talking when they could spend it loving each other.

He hadn't realised it was possible to be this happy!

Will smiled as he looked down at Lisa, lying beside him. She was fast asleep and for a moment he allowed himself the simple delight of watching her. Their love-making had been everything he could have dreamt it would be. Being able to show Lisa how he felt had been so marvellous that there weren't words to describe it. He knew that he would never forget how she had responded to him so sweetly and joyously.

Her eyelids suddenly flickered and he bent and kissed her gently on the mouth. 'Happy Christmas, sweetheart.'

'Happy Christmas to you, too,' she murmured sleepily. She dragged her hand through her tousled hair and yawned. 'What time is it?'

'Just gone eight.' He rolled her over so they were facing each other and kissed the tip of her nose. 'So how do you feel this morning? Do you still love me?'

'Mmm, I'm not sure…' She gasped when he tickled her ribs. 'OK, I give in! Yes, I love you. I love you heaps and heaps and then a whole lot more. Is that what you wanted to hear?'

'Yep. So long as you promise to start each day by telling me that you love me, I'll be satisfied,' he assured her.

'That's a very easy promise to make and stick to.' She kissed him lightly on the mouth then smiled at him. 'I don't think I shall ever grow tired of telling you that I love you, Will.'

'Me, too,' he whispered, pulling her close. He sighed as he nuzzled her hair. 'I'm so happy that it hurts, Lisa. I feel as though I want to shout it from the rooftops and tell everyone what's happened. I want the whole world to know that you're mine!'

'It's such a wonderful feeling, isn't it? And it's even better that it should have happened at Christmas. It makes it even more special in a funny sort of way.'

'It does.' He kissed her lightly on the lips then tossed back the quilt.

'Where are you going?' she demanded, leaning up on one elbow to watch him.

'I'm getting your present, of course.' He opened the dresser drawer and took out the box containing the necklace, feeling a lump come to his throat. He'd never believed he would actually give her this gift and it was unbearably poignant to be able to do so.

'Happy Christmas, darling,' he said softly, placing the box in her hands.

She opened the lid and he saw the delight on her face as she lifted out the necklace. 'Will, it's just gorgeous! I love it. Here, help me put it on.'

She turned so that he could fasten the clasp around her neck then slipped out of bed and went to the mirror to look at it. Will felt his body surge to life as he watched her standing there wearing nothing but the exquisite golden chain.

He got up and put his arms around her, dropping a kiss on the nape of her neck as he held her against him and let her see the effect she was having on him.

'I'm glad you like it. I wasn't sure if it would be right to give it to you, which is why I hid it away in the drawer.'

'Because you had no idea how I felt about you?' She turned in his arms and slid her arms around his waist. 'I love you, Will. I just wish I had a present like this for you. It would be a token of how I feel about you.'

'I don't need presents, Lisa,' he told her roughly. 'I don't need anything at all now that I have you. You are all I could ever want.'

There was no stopping the passion that claimed them once again. Will carried her back to bed and their love-making was just as wonderful as it had been the night before. They stayed in each other's arms a long time and might never have got up if the phone hadn't started ringing.

Will grimaced as he reached for the receiver. 'I hope this isn't a call to say I'm needed.'

He listened intently for a few minutes then sighed as he hung up. 'Do you want the good news first or the bad?'

'Mmm, the good, I think, although I honestly don't believe that anything really bad can happen on a wonderful day like this,' she declared, smiling at him with her heart in her eyes.

Will kissed her softly, loving her so much that it hurt. 'I know exactly what you mean and it really isn't anything terrible. But the good news first is that Sarah Donnelly came in to visit Liam last night and stayed. She told Sanjay that she'd left her husband. Apparently the police are going to prosecute him for what he did to the child. Sarah intends to find a place for her and Liam to live once he's well enough to leave hospital. Evidently, he's a lot better this morning so it just goes to show how powerful a force love is.'

'Oh, that's just brilliant news! I'm so pleased for him. Having his mum there with him will make all the difference.' Lisa smiled at him. 'OK, now to the bad bit. Come on, I can take it.'

'The little girl I operated on last night is giving them cause for concern,' he explained.

'Sanjay was very apologetic about it but he wants me to take another look at her.'

'Then you have to go,' she said firmly. She kissed him quickly then tossed back the quilt. 'I'll make some coffee while you shower.'

'I hate to leave you like this,' he began.

'Will, it doesn't matter!' She smiled at him and there was a world of love in her eyes. 'If you have to go into work, I understand. Your job is all part of the package that is Will Saunders and I wouldn't change a thing. Now, you go and do what you have to and I'll see what we've got for lunch. I'm afraid that turkey is off the menu, though. I remembered the tree but not much else!'

'I don't care what we eat so long as we're together,' he told her because it was true.

'In that case, you won't be disappointed with beans on toast,' she said, laughing at him.

Will watched her hurrying towards the kitchen then took a deep breath as the full enormity of what had happened suddenly hit him. It didn't matter how long he was gone because Lisa would be here, waiting for him, when he got back.

They would be spending Christmas at home this year.

Together.

MEDICAL ROMANCE™

Large Print

Titles for the next six months…

July

DR GRAHAM'S MARRIAGE	Meredith Webber
DOCTOR AND SON	Maggie Kingsley
FIRE RESCUE	Abigail Gordon
THE SEDUCTION CHALLENGE	Sarah Morgan

August

DEAR DOCTOR	Meredith Webber
SURGEON ON CALL	Alison Roberts
THE DOCTOR'S ADOPTION WISH	Gill Sanderson
DR MICHAELIS'S SECRET	Margaret Barker

September

THE DOCTOR'S DESTINY	Meredith Webber
THE SURGEON'S PROPOSAL	Lilian Darcy
UNDER SPECIAL CARE	Laura MacDonald
THE DOCTOR'S GIFT	Lucy Clark

MILLS & BOON®

Live the emotion

0603 LP 2P P1 Medical

MEDICAL ROMANCE™

Large Print

October

DAISY AND THE DOCTOR	Meredith Webber
THE SURGEON'S MARRIAGE	Maggie Kingsley
THE MIDWIFE'S BABY WISH	Gill Sanderson
DR DALLORI'S BRIDE	Carol Wood

November

TO THE DOCTOR: A DAUGHTER	Marion Lennox
A MOTHER'S SPECIAL CARE	Jessica Matthews
RESCUING DR MacALLISTER	Sarah Morgan
DR DEMETRIUS'S DILEMMA	Margaret Barker

December

THE SURGEON'S SECOND CHANCE	Meredith Webber
SAVING DR COOPER	Jennifer Taylor
EMERGENCY: DECEPTION	Lucy Clark
THE PREGNANT POLICE SURGEON	Abigail Gordon

MILLS & BOON®

Live the emotion

0603 LP 2P P2 Medical